❧ PLAGUE OF FROGS ❧

Plague of Frogs

by
Susan Terris

DOUBLEDAY & COMPANY, INC.
GARDEN CITY · NEW YORK
1973

ISBN: 0-385-01916-5 Trade
0-385-07770-x Prebound
Library of Congress Catalog Card Number 73–79720

FOR MYRA AND HAROLD

"There are more things in heaven and earth, Horatio,
Than are dreamt of in your philosophy."

WILLIAM SHAKESPEARE
Hamlet, Act I, v, 166–167

PLAGUE OF FROGS

Chapter 1

Jo SQUEEZED HER EYES SHUT the moment they touched upon the legless pencil vendor who sat on a low wooden wagon outside the bus station.

"What did you do that for?" her mother asked opening the door.

"Do what?" Jo asked a few seconds later as they walked toward the ticket window.

"Close your eyes like that."

"Oh, I don't know," Jo answered, hunching her shoulders slightly as she looked down into her mother's face. But she knew. On the morning of a tennis match, everything had to be calm and pleasant. The jarring sight of a legless peddler must not be allowed to disturb her sense of well-being.

It was a Saturday morning in February and Jo Massie was about to catch a Greyhound to Webster Groves for a day of preseason competition. She was wearing a tennis dress and a clean white sweatsuit with a jumping frog sewn on the front pocket. In her hand she was swinging a canvas bag and a pair of identical rackets.

She smiled as she walked through the station. She had a hunch this was going to be a good day. Everything had gone well so far. She hadn't overslept, hadn't wakened Grampa. She and her mother were here at the bus depot with plenty of time to spare. They would even have time for a cup of hot chocolate together before Jo boarded the bus. Now, if she could just manage to win her matches, everything would be perfect.

As Jo and her mother sat waiting for the mugs of chocolate to cool, they chatted idly.

"It was supposed to rain again today," Caryl Massie said, "but it seems to have cleared up."

Jo nodded. "I guess I was lucky," she answered, looking around at the early-morning travelers. She felt relaxed. No one here inside seemed as threatening as the legless man outside. "Look over there, Ma, at the lady with all those children. What do you think she's doing here at seven-thirty in the morning? And that old wino with his bottle wrapped in a brown bag. Does he think we don't know it's a bottle?"

Jo turned back toward her mother. "You could probably find a whole week's worth of stories for your TV show if you hung around the depot for the morning. If you could stand it. Everything here always seems so dirty, so ugly. . . ."

Mrs. Massie smiled as she pushed absent-mindedly at her owlish black glasses. "Compassion, my dear daughter. I agree with Grampa when he says you seem to have too little. You have plenty of curiosity, but you're a little short on compassion."

Jo laughed. "Isn't it a little too early in the morning for such B.S.? Anyway, if I have too little, you have too much. I know it's part of your job to be interested in people, but you overdo it. You're always letting people use you."

Mrs. Massie sighed. "I suppose you're right about me. And as for you—well, for fourteen you're not a bad kid. But sometimes I think that private school

2

fosters these supercilious attitudes. I wonder if I did the right thing when I put you into Ladue Hall."

Jo ignored her mother's last remarks. "Look over there," she said, pointing her finger, "just outside the coffee shop. See that heavy girl? The one in pink with the bony knees and bushy hair? She probably hasn't combed that hair in a week. What do you think she's doing carrying her quilt through the bus station?"

"Why don't you ask her?" Mrs. Massie suggested.

"Sarcasm will get you nowhere," Jo said. As she was speaking, the girl turned toward them. Jo's face lit up. "Look at her sweatshirt. It says DANVILLE. That's where they're having all the problems with the frogs. Do you think she knows anything about frogs?"

"If you're so curious, why don't you ask?"

"Well, maybe I will. I might. . . ." Jo's voice trailed off. As she was speaking, she suddenly realized that a large strawberry-colored birthmark covered most of one side of the girl's face. The unsightly stain extended from her chin up her cheek and almost around her left eye. Abruptly, Jo turned away. She stood up. "I've had enough cocoa, at least enough to take the skin off the roof of my mouth. I'm going to the ladies'. I'll meet you at the gate in a few minutes."

Jo blotted out all memory of the girl's face as she had blotted out the image of the legless vendor. Her sense of calm returned. As she was washing her hands a few minutes later, she felt fine. She smiled at her reflection in the plate-glass mirror. She saw herself

3

tall, thin, and slightly stoop-shouldered. Her protruding teeth displayed a set of expensive silver bands. Well, at least she had good hair. Her hair was her only vanity. It hung down her back long, straight, and red-blond. This morning it was tied back with a ribbon—a green one to match the frog on the pocket of her sweatsuit.

She untied the ribbon and fished a comb out of her pocket. Gently she pulled the comb through the long, fine strands of hair. Then she realized that there was someone behind her. It was the girl with the birthmark.

She tried to avoid looking at the girl's face in the mirror, but as she began to retie the ribbon, she couldn't help noticing that the girl was behaving in a very peculiar manner. She was edging slowly down the double row of pay toilets, peering first to one side and then to the other. Behind her she dragged a battered cardboard suitcase and her quilt.

Jo stared into the mirror wondering what the girl was planning to do. Then she understood. The girl was going to crawl under one of the pay stalls to use the toilet.

Her body was bulky and awkward in its loose-fitting shift and sweatshirt. Instead of crawling through headfirst, she was trying to back under and drag the suitcase and quilt after her.

Jo shook her head. The girl probably didn't want to waste a dime to get in, but couldn't she wait long enough to catch hold of an open door as someone came out? There she was squatting down, dragging her whole body backward along the dirty floor. And it looked as if the girl would never make it under the door.

Jo turned around again. "Would you like a dime?" she asked, leaning down to catch a glimpse of the face under the mop of wild hair.

"Leave me be," the girl said. "You can't help."

Jo straightened up, but she kept right on watching. The girl bumped her head twice before she realized that she would have to flatten herself out to fit underneath. At last she stretched out on the dirty tile floor. Then slowly and awkwardly she crawled under the partition. Next Jo saw two impatient hands reach out and yank at the suitcase. Jo frowned. She couldn't understand why the girl didn't just unlock the door and pick up the case.

When Jo had finished with her hair, she saw that the girl was still tugging fruitlessly at the suitcase. So, on her way to rejoin her mother, she paused long enough to straighten it out and push it up under the stall. "There," she said.

"Thanks," came the muffled reply.

"You're welcome," Jo called.

"And you should have seen her all wedged backward," Jo told her mother. "Do you suppose she'll crawl out the same way? She didn't even want the dime I . . ."

"Look, there she is again," Mrs. Massie interrupted. "Poor girl, she looks like she's been crying."

"Maybe."

Jo and her mother watched as the girl put down her belongings and placed a nickel in a peanut machine. She turned the chrome handle. The peanuts

5

came sliding down the chute and went bouncing onto the floor.

"She didn't know to put her hand there to catch them," Jo whispered. "She really is dumb."

"Isn't it time for you to board, Josie?"

"No, let's wait. Here, I'll offer her a nickel for some more peanuts."

But, before Jo could step forward, the girl dropped awkwardly to her knees and began crawling around after the peanuts. She reached for them with her left hand and stored them in her right fist. After a minute or so, she seemed to feel she had collected enough. She sat on the floor and appeared to be counting the nuts. Then she lurched to her feet, sat down on her suitcase, and began to munch the peanuts one by one.

"Disgusting," Jo said.

"Come on now, Jo. We must stop staring at her. We're being very rude."

"She's too fat for peanuts anyway," Jo commented.

"Maybe that's her breakfast. And she's not really fat. She looks to me more like she might be pregnant," Mrs. Massie said. "Maybe I should ask her if she needs help."

"And then make a TV story out of it, huh? 'Starving Pregnant Girl Found in Greyhound Depot.'"

While they were whispering, the girl suddenly rose to her feet. She came forward toward Jo, dragging her suitcase and quilt with one hand. She kept on walking until she was standing squarely in front of Jo. Then she spoke. "You," she cried, shaking her fist. "Can't you find no one else to look at? What makes you evil-eye me? Why? Because of this?" she

6

asked, pressing her hand against her strawberry-colored cheek.

Jo turned to her mother for assistance, but Mrs. Massie was silent. Jo was forced to speak for herself. "No, no, of course not. I wasn't staring at your face. Not your face," she said with a nervous little laugh. "Well . . . well . . . it's your sweatshirt. It says DANVILLE and I'm interested in Danville because I'm interested in frogs. You know all the problems they're having near Danville with frogs."

As Jo was speaking, the girl dropped her things and threw both hands up against her ears. "No frogs. Don't you talk frogs to me. And I ain't from Danville. Them frogs are bad. Bad from the Devil. Myrtle says they're a plague. A plague on all our houses!" Her voice rose higher and higher until she was shrieking.

Jo turned back to her mother. "This is weird. Come on. I'm going to the bus. This is crazy. Just crazy."

"I am not," the heavy girl shouted, throwing herself toward Jo. "I ain't crazy." She grabbed Jo by the neck. Stunned, Jo stumbled backward and fell. The girl fell with her. Before Jo could react, the girl was shaking her and pulling at her hair.

Mrs. Massie bent down and tried to force them apart. "Girls! Come on, girls. What's going on here? Stop it, Jo."

Jo pulled herself out from under the other girl. "Me? She's the one who started it."

"I did not," the girl said. "She started up with them frogs."

Mrs. Massie took the girl by the shoulder. "What's your name?" she asked. There was no answer. The

7

girl just sat there glaring at Jo. Mrs. Massie stood up. She picked up the quilt and began to fold it carefully. "How beautiful," she said. "It's handmade. Did you do it yourself?"

"No," the girl answered shortly. "It was Myrtle."

Mrs. Massie took hold of the girl's hand very gently. "Now tell me. What's your name?"

"Marcella."

"Just Marcella?"

"Marcella Fishencor."

Mrs. Massie nodded. "Well, Marcella, I'm Caryl Massie and this is my daughter Jo." She turned back toward Jo. "Marcella's things have spilled all over, Josie. Will you help her put them back?"

Jo looked around at the contents of the suitcase tumbled there on the floor. A dress, a sweater, underwear, hair curlers, and a book that looked like a Bible. "Yeah, I'll help," she agreed. "You get my case and rackets and I'll help the girl."

"Her name is Marcella."

"Okay, I'll help *Marcella*," Jo said with a grimace. She sat up on her knees and began gathering the scattered things together and stuffing them back in the suitcase.

"Where's my buckeye?" Marcella said fearfully.

"What buckeye?"

"My lucky one."

Jo wasn't particularly concerned about lucky buckeyes. She shut her mouth tightly and looked over at Marcella. The ugly birthmark even made the girl's left eye appear smaller than the right one. Jo glanced down at her watch. The bus for Webster Groves would be leaving in five minutes, and here she was

8

picking up clothes that belonged to some crazy country girl. At this same moment, something else occurred to Jo. She looked down at her sweatsuit. Her immaculate white outfit was now all smudged with bus-station grime, highlighted by purple stains from someone's spilled popsicle. As she tried halfheartedly to brush herself clean, she suddenly felt very angry.

She should have known it. Any morning that included a legless peddler and a girl with a strawberry birthmark was just not going to be *her* day.

"Help Marcella find the buckeye, Josie. It's very important to her."

"Who cares about some old buckeye?" Jo asked, making no effort to conceal her annoyance. As she was speaking, however, she caught sight of it. There it was—brown, round, and satiny—resting behind the edge of a trash can. Jo stared at it blankly for a moment. Then, with a small, unobtrusive gesture, she reached for the buckeye. For some perverse reason, she was in no hurry to return it.

"You evil-eyed me," Marcella said accusingly. "You talked frogs and now my lucky buckeye's gone!" She was sobbing, and quite a crowd was beginning to collect. It was turning into a real scene. And Jo wasn't up to it. Not this morning.

She looked down once more at her soiled clothes. Then, making up her mind, she stood up and took the canvas bag and rackets from her mother. But she didn't offer the buckeye to Marcella. After all, why did she need that buckeye? She seemed like a silly, superstitious girl. She'd be better off without it.

Jo would keep the buckeye. Maybe it *was* lucky.

After the morning she'd had, she could use a little luck.

"Listen, Ma," Jo said, "I'm going to have to run if I want to make my bus. Thanks for the ride." Then, clutching her bag, two rackets, and one satiny, brown buckeye, she trotted off to board the bus.

Chapter 2

꒰꒰꒰ THE DOORBELL AT THE MASSIE HOUSE was ringing. Someone very impatient was jabbing at it over and over again. Not more than ten feet from the front door, Jo sat staring into a terrarium, watching her bullfrogs splash in their bowl of water. A frown indicated that she had heard the bell, but she made no effort to answer it.

"The bell. The bell," a gruff voice echoed down the hall. That was Grampa. "Someone. Anyone. Johanna," he shouted. "Someone, before my ears fall off."

Jo still didn't move. She dangled a mealy worm in the terrarium and watched the frogs jump for it. The ringing continued. At last, there was a shuffling sound from the kitchen. "I'm a coming. Hold your horses. It's always for Jo. Someone name of Ellen or Kendall."

A heavy girl in faded pink cotton came out of the kitchen and went toward the front door. Jo glanced up disdainfully. Marcella Fishencor was an appalling, ignorant girl. She'd been staying with the Massies for two weeks already, and Jo still couldn't stand her. Jo shook her head. This morning, Marcella looked worse than usual. She was wearing wooden clogs and her already curly hair was done up in rollers.

"Who is it?" Marcella called, pressing her face against the unopened door.

11

"Roger Frey," a voice shouted.

Marcella turned the handle and flung the door open. "Can't you wait? What makes you in such a hurry?" she scolded. "Are you the boy going tennis playing with Jo?"

Jo listened to this exchange, but she hadn't yet bothered to look up. Her mother—her compassionate mother—had arranged for a boy named Roger Frey to travel with her to Springfield for this week's matches. And Jo wasn't very happy about it. If she had wanted a traveling companion, she'd have arranged it herself.

"Listen, Jo," Marcella called out. "Can't you ever get the door? Why do I have to do everything around here? Dishes, scrubbing bathrooms, laundry. And you —you can't even pull open the door. This is your boy standing here and he sure is a small one. I think you ought to throw him back."

"Shut up, Marcella," Jo snapped. "Come in, Roger. I'm Jo." Jo turned toward Marcella. "Listen, Marcella, he's no boyfriend and he's small because he's only twelve. Or is it eleven?"

"Thirteen," Roger answered.

"Thirteen. And I'm lucky enough to be his chaperone for the day."

Roger stood in the doorway with a wide grin spread across his face. "Say, this place is really something. First it takes fifteen minutes to get someone to answer the door, and then all I get is insults. You two are quite a pair. Did you ever consider going on stage?"

Jo bent down to smooth out her socks. Then, instead of answering Roger, she stared at him. Marcella was right. He was a small one. He was short and stocky, with shaggy brown hair. His white clothes made his slightly olive skin look tanned. In his arms he carried an old, rolled-up gym sweatsuit and a battered-looking racket. He didn't seem to want to stand still. He kept shifting his weight from one foot to the other.

While Jo was staring, Roger did a little gawking of his own, squinting slightly as he looked from one girl to the other. "Are you two sisters?" he asked at last.

"Oh, sure," Jo said. "She's my pregnant, unmarried, sixteen-year-old sister. No, of course she's not my sister. Hardly! My mother picked her up in the Greyhound station two weeks ago. She's from some little town in the Ozarks, and she's going to stay here working for us until her baby comes, in June."

Marcella turned abruptly. "Don't you evil-eye my baby," she warned. "You can't talk about her. You and your frogs. You even keeps them in the house so I have to look away when I come in here. Least they're out from the bedroom now. That's one good thing. They can't give me bad dreams no more. Frogs are a plague. A plague on all our houses. And you're no good, Jo Massie. Only Grampa and your mama. They're good. They care."

Instead of answering Marcella's tirade, Jo changed the subject. "Hey, Marcella, what are those dirty wool socks doing tied around your neck?" she asked.

"Even I know that," Roger said. "That's an old cure for sore throats."

Marcella smiled broadly. "Right! Can't never cure

13

a sore throat without them." She seemed pleased to have someone agreeing with her for a change.

Jo looked at Roger angrily. "Every day, she comes up with some crazy new home remedy. I don't need you here to encourage her."

Marcella twisted her hands together and clattered her wooden clogs against the floor. "What do you know? There are more things on heaven and earth than are dreamt of in your philosophy."

For a moment, Jo sat there. Then she began to laugh. "Why, that's from *Hamlet!* Only you left out the 'Horatio.' Those aren't your words. They're Shakespeare's!"

"No, Myrtle's," Marcella said. "She reads Shakespeare. She and my father was part of the Goose Creek Chatauqua Theater."

"Oh, tell me more," Jo said. "Tell me about Myrtle and about your father. You never tell us anything."

"No," Marcella said with a pout. "I ain't going to say nothing."

Jo looked over at Roger. He was laughing, but she got the distinct impression that he was laughing at both of them and not just at Marcella.

"I ain't going to have you laughing at me and not at my cures neither," Marcella said, fingering the wool socks wrapped around her neck. "They work, my cures do. I learned 'em from Myrtle."

Jo glared first at Roger and then back at Marcella. "You and your cures," she scoffed. "If they work, why didn't you ever find a cure . . . a cure to take the mark off your face?"

Jo held her breath. She half expected that Marcella would jump on her as she had done that day at the bus station. But she didn't. She just frowned. "My daddy tried," she said. "He wanted me to get beautiful. Myrtle told him he might cure that mark by making me touch a dead man's hand. I wasn't but a baby when he made me touch someone dead. Maybe it was the wrong dead man, 'cause that was one cure that never worked."

"Do you really believe in cures like that?" Jo asked.

"Don't know," Marcella said, turning away. "Maybe." Then, with a shrug, she clumped back toward the kitchen.

As soon as she was gone, Roger spoke. "Why did you have to ask her about that mark?"

Jo leaned her head to one side. "I don't know. I just felt like it."

Roger looked toward the kitchen. "Why didn't she get an abortion?" he asked.

"You're pretty hip for thirteen, aren't you?"

"I asked you a question."

Jo nodded her head. "Because she didn't want one. She has some crazy idea that she's going to keep the baby, too. Sit down, will you, and stop all that jiggling around?"

Roger dropped the sweatsuit, racket, and himself into the nearest chair. "Who's the baby's father?" he asked.

"We don't have the faintest idea," Jo said. "You saw how she clammed up. We're curious, but she just won't talk. My mother got us all into this. She knows someone for every problem. For Marcella it's some group called the Sisters of Hope. They have a hospital for unmarried girls, but someone else has to provide them with room and board until they have their babies. And, thanks to my mother, we're stuck with Marcella for three months."

"Then what?"

"Who knows? Who cares? Listen, you don't know what it's like with her around here. No peace or privacy. Everywhere I go, she's there—watching, listening. Even the meals are awful, now that she's doing most of the cooking. We eat what *she* likes. Mostly beans. Also forty-three varieties of squash. Ever had squash soup? How about squash pie with brown sugar and marshmallows on top?"

"So, who did all the cooking and cleaning before she came?" Roger asked.

Jo shrugged. "Ma did. And I helped."

"Then, what do you have to complain about? You're talking like some kind of spoiled brat."

"Oh, shut up," Jo said. "I didn't ask for your opinion."

Their conversation was interrupted by the tapping of Grampa's cane. "Hello, Gramp," Jo said, standing up as he came into the living room. "This is Roger Frey. My grandfather, Mr. Grunik. Roger and I are taking the bus to the tennis matches together."

Slowly, Grampa made his way into the room. He was a short, chesty man with a crown of white hair. He limped slightly as he walked. He was smiling up at Roger as he lowered himself carefully into a hard-backed wooden chair. "Glad to see you, son. Anyone who lives in a houseful of women like I do is always grateful for a little male companionship." With a wink, Grampa turned to Jo. "Aren't you glad to have traveling company today?"

"Oh, sure I am, Grampa," she replied mechanically.

"Then why'd you act so bitchy to him and to Marcella before I came in the room?"

Jo slid her hand down one red-blond braid and laughed self-consciously.

Roger stepped forward and shook hands with Grampa. "Mr. Grunik, I'm glad to know you. You have my sympathy."

Grampa laughed. But Jo backed away. She was not amused. Anyway, it was time to go. "If you're ready, Roger, we'll leave now," she said sharply. "First we catch the bus from Ladue into St. Louis. Then the Greyhound. Grampa, tell Marcella I won't be here for dinner. Or Ma either. She'll meet us at the depot at nine-thirty. Will you remember all that, Grampa?"

"Sure, I'll remember. And stop talking to me like I'm some dimwit. Good-by, Roger. Maybe you'll come back and play cards with me some afternoon. And good luck; I'll keep my fingers crossed for you both."

Chapter 3

 JO MADE LITTLE ATTEMPT to carry on a conversation with Roger during their trip. He annoyed her because he never sat still. He kept wiggling and tapping his fingers together. The Greyhound driver had asked her to keep her little brother's ticket for him. If this advice bothered Roger, who barely came up to Jo's shoulder, he didn't let on. But it did irritate Jo. She no more wanted Roger mistaken for her brother than she wanted Marcella mistaken for her sister. She was the only one. She and Ma and Grampa were the whole family. And she liked it the way it was.

As the bus rolled along, she closed her eyes and tried to rest. Somehow, images of Marcella Fishencor kept floating through her head. Marcella's face with its ugly birthmark. Marcella's sloppy dresses and coarsely tangled hair. Marcella trying to wring out the mop without bending over. Sleeping with a Bible under her pillow to ward off nightmares. Wiping the bathroom mirror with old pieces of newspaper. Turning her clogs upside down by the bed to prevent foot cramps. Taking the rugs outside to shake them instead of using the vacuum. And then coming in with the dust all over her clothes. Jo chuckled.

"Did you say something?" Roger asked.

"No, I was just thinking," she answered. Jo was

18

disgusted with herself. Even away from home, Marcella was intruding on her privacy. She could hear Marcella's voice nagging her to keep the newspapers off the floor, to pick up her pajamas, to fold her towel. Just remembering made Jo feel indignant. After all, it was *her* room, not Marcella's. She had given in to her mother's pleas—allowed Marcella to sleep in the extra bed in her room. Use two drawers in her dresser, hang up clothes in her closet.

But that girl was so ignorant. So slow. It seemed like the only thing she knew how to do was clean a house. How could she be so fanatic about cleaning a house, Jo wondered, and yet so sloppy about the way she dressed? Marcella's only feeble attempt at self-improvement was her effort to curl her mass of coarse hair.

And that smell. "A little deodorant would help," Jo kept telling her.

"Nothing wrong with the smell of good, clean, honest sweat," Marcella always answered.

"Nothing wrong with the smell of sweat?" Jo mused.

"What's your problem?" Roger asked. "Why do you keep talking to yourself?"

Jo laughed self-consciously. "Oh, I was just thinking about Marcella—about what a slob she is. Perspires all the time and never bothers to wash or use any deodorant."

"Oh, I feel sorry for you. So sorry for poor little Jo. What about Marcella? She's the one who's pregnant. She's the one with the awful birthmark on her face. She didn't look dirty to me. I didn't smell anything. Don't you feel sorry for her? Not even a little bit?"

Jo turned and looked out the window. She wasn't going to answer Roger. She'd just ignore him.

As the bus was approaching the outskirts of Springfield, Roger spoke again. "You know," he said quietly, "you may be older and bigger than I am, but you're no smarter. Your size, your age, your intelligence—they don't give you special rights to insult people. I didn't ask to come with you today. That was your mother's idea. And you don't have to treat me like I'm some kind of worm. Or her either—that Marcella. Even if she doesn't use the proper kind of deodorant."

Jo looked down at him. "I don't need you to give me lectures. You're arrogant!"

"I suppose you're not," Roger shot back. "You're arrogant and supercilious."

Jo cocked one eyebrow. "Oh, supercilious! That's one of my mother's pet words. You use it, but I bet you don't even know what it means. . . ."

Roger strummed his fingers against the strings of his tennis racket. "Oh, I think· I do," he said with a yawn. "It comes from Latin—*super* and *cilia*. It means raising the eyebrows at everything, just like you're doing."

"How do you know that?" Jo demanded.

"Easy. My father's a professor of Greek and Latin at the University. And, as I said before, you may be older and bigger, but I'm just as smart." Roger was grinning at her as she spoke.

Reluctantly, she yielded and grinned back at him.

"Okay," she said, "you're just as smart. At least for today. I don't want to argue any more. I was wrong and you were right to tell me off. So I'll try to be nicer. Okay?"

About an hour later, Jo and Roger were sitting in the bleachers near the tournament desk holding paper cups filled with hot coffee. The coffee wasn't for drinking. They were merely holding the cups to warm their fingers and ward off the early-morning chill. They had already checked in. Now they both had time to waste. Roger's first match was scheduled for eleven, and Jo wouldn't be playing hers until noon.

Jo was eying the other players and their parents. "Look at them," she scoffed.

"At who?" Roger asked, craning his neck.

"All the uptight parents promoting their children. I'm glad my mother doesn't come. And why do the *parents* wear their tennis whites? They aren't playing. It's all part of the mystique, isn't it?" Jo shook her head and looked over at Roger. "Have you ever thought how stupid this all is? Wear white, follow the rules, don't step on the line."

Roger stopped tapping his feet and looked over at Jo. "I thought you liked tennis."

"Oh, I do," she said. "It suits me. I'm competitive. I like to win. I'm good at it. It's just that the tournaments are beginning to get me down. This must be your first one."

Roger nodded.

"Then I'd better break you in. You might as well learn right away that you don't win matches just with your playing skills. You've got to use a lot of psychology to win at a tournament. You've got to psych out your opponent. By keeping your sweatsuit on, for instance."

Roger looked puzzled. "Just what does that do?"

"That shows him you think it will be such an easy match that you're not taking off your sweatsuit, because you don't expect to be on the court long enough to warm up."

Roger grinned. "And I thought I could just play well and trust to my lucky fisheyes." From his pocket, he produced a pair of grayish-white stones, which he said were the boiled eyeballs of a catfish.

Jo laughed. "You sound just like Marcella! Do you really believe in that superstitious stuff?"

"Don't you?" Roger asked. "At least a little?"

She shrugged. "I found a buckeye once that was supposed to be lucky. But after I lost two matches in a row, I threw it away."

"Well, I'm going to keep my fisheyes," Roger said, "even if they aren't any good." He paused and leaned forward. "But I interrupted you. Maybe you have some more advice for me."

Jo took a sip of coffee. It tasted terrible. She spat it out. "Oh, you'll learn fast enough. Remember how smart you are? Now, do me a favor."

"What?"

"Get lost. I'd like to use this time to think."

"I'll be quiet," Roger said, sliding his sturdy frame a few feet farther down the bench.

"I doubt it. Now, beat it, will you?"

"Yeah, I will, but look at this: I've only had these

tennis shoes six weeks and I've already got a hole in the right toe."

"The serving toe," Jo commented. "I always have that problem, too. Now, go away."

Roger didn't move. "Have you ever wondered what happens to all the good left-footed tennis shoes when all the right ones have holes from serving? Maybe I could open a left-footed shoe store for tennis players with two left feet!"

Jo laughed in spite of herself.

Roger stretched a white sweatband Indian style around his shaggy hair. Then he squinted at her. "Listen, a little while ago, you were talking about the mystique of tennis and I wanted to ask you about your two matching rackets. Aren't they part of the mystique?"

Jo looked down at her identical rackets. Was Roger laughing at her again? "Of course not," she answered. "You have to have a second racket in case a string breaks. No one can play with a broken string. Just what will you do if you get a broken string?"

"Why, I'll play with it. I saw Isaac Stern once playing the violin with a broken string. If he can do it with a violin, I can do it with a tennis racket."

Jo laughed again. "You have an answer for everything! You're funny. But it's distracting. Keeps me from concentrating. Why don't you stop all this talking and joking and try thinking about your tennis game? And let me think about mine."

"What kind of thinking?" Roger asked.

"About winning! About your opponent. Or—if

you're really hard up—reach into your pocket and think about your lucky fisheyes."

Neither lucky fisheyes nor psyching out the opponent worked for Roger. He lost his first match. Jo didn't fare much better. She was eliminated in round two.

"Let's find someplace to eat," Jo suggested glumly. "The next bus doesn't leave for ages. Some place good. I could use a good dinner to cheer me up—and some relief from Marcella's cooking. A steak sandwich, maybe."

Two blocks from the bus station, they found an old railroad dining car that had been converted into a restaurant. A hand-painted sign in its window caught Roger's eye. It said: TODAY'S SPECIAL—POSSUM STEW, 99¢.

"Are you an adventurous eater?" Roger asked as they stood there outside the diner.

Jo wasn't sure she was, but she really didn't want to admit it to him. "Sure," she agreed. "Let's try it."

Together they climbed up the metal stairs and slid the door open. The steamy interior felt good after the cool air outside. For a moment, the place seemed to be empty; then a beaming face peered up over the counter followed by a small body, much too small for the size of the round, shiny face with the upswept hairdo. "Hello there, I've got some customers. Some tennis kids from the city. Welcome. You are my guests and I am Miss Sapiro."

Jo backed up. She was unnerved by the woman's size and the width of her face. She was a dwarf, almost. Jo was leery of Roger's choice. Leery of the woman and of the fact that there were no other customers. She was angry with herself for following his suggestion. Roger was bright and he had a good sense of humor, but he *was* younger. Jo was supposed to be in charge. She didn't have to eat here just because *he* felt adventurous.

She wanted to speak up and insist that they find some ordinary coffee shop to eat in. But Roger was halfway across the diner already. It was too late. It would make a scene if they left now. Embarrass them. Hurt the woman's feelings.

Jo glanced around. She wasn't interested in having dinner in an old railroad car attended by a dwarf. She wasn't looking for adventure. Only for a steak sandwich. "Next time," she told herself, "next time, I'll know better."

Chapter 4

⧂⧂⧂ "COME IN, COME IN," Miss Sapiro insisted, trotting over to them on a pair of tiny feet. "You don't want to sit at the counter. I'll give you a table. A table for the pretty redhead and her little brother. You need a haircut, sonny. How can you see to hit a tennis ball, huh?"

Before Jo could offer any objections, Miss Sapiro had them seated at a table with a flowered plastic cloth. "What does possum meat taste like?" Roger asked her.

"Like chicken dark meat," she said, her shining face nodding up and down.

"Well, make that possum for me," Roger said firmly. "What about you, Jo? You want the same?"

Jo didn't want the same. Her mother always said she was curious and she was. But evidently she was not quite as curious as Roger Frey. Yet, somehow, she felt she had to prove something to him, so she nodded. "Sure. Make that two specials."

Miss Sapiro hurried off. She disappeared behind a partition into the kitchen. Jo and Roger sat in silence. Jo looked around the diner again. Well, at least it was clean. And that woman was very pleasant, Jo decided, even if she was a little deformed.

Roger stared at Jo across the table. "Don't you want to know anything about me?" he asked abruptly.

"Sure. What do you want to tell me?" Jo replied, amused by his earnestness.

"Well," he said quickly, "I'm interested in naval history. I build model ships out of balsa wood. I play the piano—Russian music mostly. My father's a teacher, like I told you. Mom's a speech therapist. And I have a brother Chris. He's seventeen. They're all okay, my family. I like them."

He paused for breath. Then he started right in again. "I'm a year ahead in school. Public school. That puts me in ninth grade. I ice-skate in the winter and play tennis in the summer. Oh yes— and I'm interested in dreams, in the meanings of dreams. Do you dream a lot?"

Jo nodded.

"Do you write them down and then try to figure out what they mean?" Roger asked.

"Of course not."

"Well, I do," he said. "You should try it. You'd find out a lot about yourself." He pointed one finger at Jo. "But, go on; it's your turn now. Tell me about you. What's important to you? Is tennis important?"

Jo smiled. She leaned her elbows on the table. "No, tennis isn't that important. Not like it is to some people. It's just a game. I'll never be a champion. I haven't the dedication or concentration."

"Well, what *is* important? My father always tries to get me to figure out what's *really* important. Is that fancy girls' school you go to important? Do you like dancing around Maypoles in fancy white dresses? Isn't that the big deal of the year at Ladue Hall—the Maypole? Come on, now, tell me what's important."

"That's a hard question," Jo said. "I don't always think much about what I do. I just do it. And mostly I like what I do."

"And you like yourself?"

Jo nodded. "Sure. Why not?" She unfolded a paper napkin and arranged it in her lap. "Having time to myself—that's important. I do a lot of modern dance. I like dancing—even Maypole dancing at Ladue Hall. It's a good school for me. I have a few good friends, but I stick to myself a lot. Probably because I'm so close to Ma. And Grampa. My father lives in Spain. I haven't seen him since I was three."

Jo twisted the salt shaker between her fingers. "But things are good at home," she said. "At least they were before Marcella came. I don't like her hanging around the house all the time, sharing my room. Oh, yes, I'm a year ahead in school, too. That makes me a sophomore."

"Sophomore—from the Greek *sophos* and *moros* —that makes you a wise fool. That's what those two words mean, you know."

"Show-off."

Roger grinned. "What about the frogs?" he asked, changing the subject. "You have some special attachment to frogs. You keep them in your living room and you even have one on your sweatsuit."

"Oh, it's just an interest. When I was little, I collected stuffed frogs and pretended that they were good luck. Now I study live ones. My science teacher—Mr. Bassett—helps me do some frog surgery. I think I might be interested in studying medicine."

"You know about the troubles they're having in the Ozarks, near Danville?"

Jo nodded. "That's how I met Marcella, actually. Her sweatshirt said DANVILLE. No, I don't know anything special. Mostly just what I read in the papers. The Smithsonian sent a team of observers, and they haven't called it a plague yet. They're just investigating." As Jo was speaking, she accidentally turned over the salt.

"Quick," said Roger, "throw a pinch over your left shoulder."

Jo laughed. "Silly superstition. You're sounding like Marcella again."

"Well," he said defensively, "you're superstitious about tennis, aren't you? At least you admitted it earlier today."

"Did I say that? Well, maybe I am. But it's more like a game I play with myself than real superstition."

As they were talking about superstitions, Miss Sapiro trotted out of the kitchen carrying two huge steaming plates, each covered with brown lumps swimming in a gooey gravy.

"Two possum specials," she sang out. Her voice reverberated off the metal walls of the diner.

Jo swallowed hard when she looked down at the heaping plate Miss Sapiro put in front of her. Why had she let Roger blackmail her into trying possum meat just because he was going to?

Little Miss Sapiro was saying something. Jo looked over at the woman's broad, perspiring face. "I was asking if either of you wanted catsup for your possum."

"Catsup?" Jo gasped. She looked across at Roger. He, too, was struggling not to laugh. "No catsup," she managed to say. "I'm sure we'll love it just like it is."

Miss Sapiro patted Jo on the head. "Bless you," she said. "Now eat and enjoy. I've been waiting all afternoon for someone to order possum meat. It's the first time."

"First time what?" Jo asked.

"First time I ever stewed possum. My nephew brought him to me all skinned. Now eat up and enjoy it. If your plates aren't cleaned, I'll go in the corner and cry my eyes out."

As soon as Miss Sapiro went bustling back to the kitchen area, Jo and Roger began to snicker.

"It's your fault," said Jo.

Roger just grinned. "Dig in," he advised. "Before it gets cold. After you—ladies first."

Jo thrust her fork tentatively at one of the half-submerged lumps. "It's fighting me back," she whispered. "I can't even get the fork into it. Oh, there it goes." Jo stuck the fork in her mouth and bit into the possum meat. She'd never tasted anything like that. It tasted acrid and it was gristly. She blinked rapidly to keep her eyes from watering. But she didn't make a face or say a word to Roger. After pretending to chew the morsel three or four times, she managed to swallow it whole. It was a large chunk and she could feel the rings of muscle in her esophagus trying to squeeze it along to the stomach.

"Well?" Roger asked, looking up from where he had been stirring his meat with a fork.

"Go ahead," Jo urged. "Try it. I wouldn't want to spoil it for you by telling you how it tastes."

Roger scooped up several lumps of meat with his

fork. After all, she had tried it first. Now he seemed determined to show that he was as adventurous as he had claimed. Without further delay, he shoveled the heaping forkful into his mouth. Right in the middle of the first bite, he choked.

"What's the matter?" Jo asked solicitously. "Aren't you an adventurous eater?"

"This stuff is abominable," Roger sputtered, one cheek distended with the evil-tasting, unchewable stuff. "She said it tasted like chicken. How did you ever swallow it?"

"Whole," Jo said. "And try a little water."

Jo and Roger stared at each other across the table. "Now what?" Roger asked. "I have an idea. No, forget it. You think of something. They must teach you how to handle these delicate social situations at Ladue Hall."

"Let's leave our dollar ninety-eight and sneak out," said Jo quickly.

"Can't," Roger said. "Here she comes."

"How's everything with my little tennis players?" she sang out as she minced down the aisle toward them. "I haven't had a moment to taste the possum myself yet, but it's an old family recipe. Do you like it? Finish it all and I'll treat you to free dishes of my special tapioca pudding. Fisheyes and glue. That's what we used to call tapioca. Now, is there anything you need?"

Roger nodded. "Yes," he said. "Catsup and more water."

After Miss Sapiro had fetched the water and catsup, she slid the door open and sat down on the front steps, where she began to crochet on a large, tan-colored mass.

"That's probably a possum catcher," Roger cracked.

Jo looked down at her plate. Blobs of grease were beginning to congeal around the edge of the plate. "We had our chance to escape. Now we're stuck. What do we do?"

"Do you suppose she mistook a possum for a raccoon?" Roger asked. "Or . . . a prairie dog?"

"Maybe."

"God! That's it," Roger whispered. "It's probably a cat—an alley cat her nephew skinned and gave her to serve up to the unsuspecting folks from the city."

"Stop," Jo pleaded. "My stomach hurts."

"From possum meat?"

"From listening to you crack jokes. Now, look here, Roger. You got us into this! And you'd better get us out."

Roger ran his hands through his hair. "You're older. I defer to you."

"B.S. Now, think."

"Shall we pour catsup all over it and choke it down?" Roger asked.

"No!" Jo was certain that she was not going to eat another mouthful of possum—or alley cat. "Now, think!"

"Is everything all right?" Miss Sapiro called out from her seat on the steps. "Do you want another helping?"

"No, we're just fine," Roger called back with feigned cheerfulness. Then he looked over at Jo. "Okay, hand me your canvas bag."

"My bag?"

"Yes," he insisted. "We'll spoon the possum into your bag. Then we'll pay her and get out of here."

"Oh, no, Roger, not into my bag. It'll ruin it. Turn it rancid. Let's just leave."

Roger shook his head firmly. "And hurt Miss S's feelings? No; she's kind of deformed, and I feel sorry for her, like I do for that girl at your house."

Jo pursed her lips together. People like Marcella or Miss Sapiro always brought unpleasantness into her life. "All right," she said with a sigh. She emptied the bag and rolled its contents up in her sweatpants. She'd do as Roger suggested. Anything to avoid more possum meat.

Roger managed to prop Jo's bag between their knees under the table. Then, as nonchalantly as possible, the two began to spoon the stew into the bag. Their task was made more difficult because a family of four came into the diner. They had to eye Miss Sapiro and the new people at the same time to make sure that their efforts were unnoticed. The plastic tablecloth hampered their task. Jo could see splotches of brown gravy soaking into her tennis dress and Roger's shirt. Every time their eyes met, they had to clench their teeth together to keep from exploding with laughter.

When the last gristly lump had been spooned into the waiting bag, Jo grabbed for it and zipped it shut. Then she slung it on the chair next to her.

"What about the gravy?" Roger asked.

"Forget it," Jo advised. "Unless you want to drink *two* plates of cold possum gravy all by yourself." Jo

33

made a face. "Just think, this morning I didn't even know you. Wasn't I lucky?"

"You almost lost your chance by refusing to open the door."

"I must have had a lucky premonition," Jo said mischievously.

"I thought you weren't superstitious."

"It's just an expression."

"What about the gravy?" Roger asked again.

"You are a persistent little guy."

"References to my size are not appreciated."

"Okay," Jo said. "Come on. Let's pay now and get out. If she thinks we're really finished, we'll have to sample her tapioca pudding—her fisheyes and glue."

"Probably, made with real fisheyes," Roger said. "And real glue."

Hastily, they said their good-bys to Miss Sapiro and backed out of the diner. Gingerly, Jo carried the bag of possum chunks. "It's beginning to leak through," she said.

"Don't complain," Roger laughed. "That family in there ordered possum specials, too. And they didn't come equipped with a bag! It was all your fault anyway. You were the one who spilled the salt."

Chapter 5

ꙮꙮꙮ Jo WAS LATE getting home from school. She'd stayed to help Mr. Bassett set up a science experiment for the next day's lab session. She didn't remember that she was supposed to play tennis with Roger Frey until she was turning her key in the front door.

The friendship begun over plates of possum meat had continued despite the difference in their ages. In the month since the Springfield tournament, they'd been meeting about twice a week to play tennis at the Ladue Hall courts. It was convenient to play there, because Jo's house was only a few blocks from the school's forty-acre campus. Roger lived half a mile away from Jo, so he could come either by bicycle or on foot to meet her.

"Hello," she called out, dropping her book bag near the front door.

Instead of any real greeting, she heard a few half-hearted grunts. When she looked into the living room, she found that Roger and Grampa were engrossed in a game of blackjack. Marcella, in curlers and clogs, sat on the floor looking on. In her lap she held a bowl filled with leftover macaroni and beans. Jo shook her head as she saw Marcella dip two fingers into the bowl, scoop up a glob of cold food, and shove it into her mouth.

"Chew with your mouth shut," Jo said. "You

35

promised you'd remember." Then, looking away from Marcella, she walked up behind Roger and Grampa. "I said, 'Hello.'"

"Yeah, hi there. Hit me again," Roger said, turning back to his game. "Your grandfather is robbing me of all my bus money. All my lunch money."

"I thought we were supposed to play tennis," Jo said.

"We were," Roger answered without looking up, "but you didn't show and now I'm in the middle of a lucky streak; I may even win back some of my money."

Grampa chewed thoughtfully on the soggy end of his cigar. "Blackjack, son, is all skill. Not luck. See this. You lose again. Now, that's it for today. You mustn't disappoint Johanna. She is not known for her patience."

"So I've observed," Roger agreed.

Grampa knocked the ash off the end of his cigar. He cleared his throat and lifted up his brandy glass. "But, Johanna, before you run off, pour me a little glass of cognac, will you?"

"Let Marcella do it," Jo said. "And, besides, the doctor said you should cut down. Marcella—put away that cold mess you're eating and get him some cognac."

Marcella pouted. "She's standing there and I'm down here on the floor. Can't she do it? Anyhow, you promised you'd tell my fortune with the cards, Grampa. Remember? You know, tell me about the baby. I want you to tell me she'll come out with no mark on her face, you hear?"

Grampa nodded. "That's right. So you pour it for

me, Johanna. Marcella doesn't like to get it for me either. She thinks I should be drinking sassafras tea to thin my blood at this time of year." Grampa picked up the cards. Marcella crawled across the rug until she was by his feet. He cleared his throat. "Now, about that baby . . ."

Jo and Roger exchanged looks as the fortune-telling began.

". . . it will be born in a big hospital. See this four of hearts? Why does everyone go to the hospital now? When I was born, it was at home. That was good enough then."

Marcella nodded. "I was born at home, too. Myrtle brought me."

Jo shot another quick glance over toward Roger. "Myrtle? I thought she spent all her time making quilts and reading Shakespeare."

Marcella shook her head. "Just busywork. She does the midwifing when the doctor can't come."

"Tell us about it," Jo said.

But Marcella ignored her and turned back to Grampa and the cards.

Jo poured a snifter of cognac and tried to avoid looking at Marcella, who was dipping her fingers into the cold macaroni again. Marcella had been with them for only six weeks, but to Jo it seemed like six months. It was the little things that got to her—like this business of eating cold food from the refrigerator with her fingers or chewing with her mouth open. And the bedroom window. Marcella wouldn't sleep with it open. She insisted that the night air was poisonous.

But Ma had promised the Sisters of Hope that

37

they would provide a home for her until the baby was born. Now they had to do it. Caryl Massie was also busy searching for a job for Marcella and a place for her to live after the baby was born. It made Jo laugh. She could picture everything in her head: Marcella would clean the baby's room, curl its hair, and feed it squash and beans. That was all she knew how to do.

Jo looked over at Grampa. He was delighted to have Marcella around. He talked to her about his theory of horse racing, about wine-making in Germany when he was a boy. And then, they both liked to compare favorite home remedies. Well, Grampa was a lonely old man. He was so eager for companionship that he didn't much care who was providing the company.

"Are we still going to play?" Jo asked, eying Roger's faded jeans.

"Sure, if you want to. But don't look at me that way. I don't need whites to play at Ladue Hall. If you don't want to play, just say so and I'll go home and work on my new model."

Grampa winked at Marcella. Then he spoke to Jo. "It does my heart good to hear this Roger boy talk to you the way you talk to everyone else."

Jo was about to answer Grampa, but when she looked up, she saw her mother in the doorway. "Why, hello. I didn't know you were home. Are all the world's problems solved today?"

"Don't I wish," Mrs. Massie said, pulling two coats from the front-hall closet. "I've been back in my room working on a report on school buses. But now I'm ready for a walk with Grampa. We're looking for crocus and pussywillow."

"Think we might find any owls' eggs?" Grampa asked with a little nod of his head. "Marcella says they're a good cure for hangover. Or dandelion greens? She says she'll cook them up for me if we can find them. They're supposed to give you energy, she says."

Caryl Massie laughed. "Owls' eggs, probably not. But we might find some dandelion greens if we look. Are they really edible, Marcella? Are you sure you don't want to come along and help us find them?"

Marcella grasped a table leg and hauled herself to her feet. "No walking. I got to be careful so I don't twist up the cord and strangle the baby."

Jo was on her way to change, but she couldn't resist turning back to answer this remark. "That's what you said about cleaning off the top of the refrigerator, too. Anything you don't want to . . ."

"Enough, Josie. Come on, Grampa. Here's your coat and cane. And, Jo, the paper on the front-hall table has some more articles on frogs you might want to see."

Jo tossed the paper at Roger. "You read it. I'll be right back."

Jo wriggled out of her red-tweed school uniform and into a tennis dress. She grabbed her racket and a can of balls. Roger was lounging on the couch reading the paper when she returned.

"Listen to this," he said as he heard her approaching. "Now the toads are adding to the plague. They're singing at night in the ponds and lakes near Danville."

"Must be spadefoot toads."

"It doesn't say. Just that they're making a terrible racket that can be heard for miles, and fighting together in the ponds."

"Let me see," Jo insisted, dropping one tennis shoe. She scanned the paper quickly. "You're right. It doesn't say, but it must be spadefoot toads. Some crazy farmer near there imported thousands of them, hoping the tadpoles would eat all the mosquito larvae. I read about that last fall. First the frogs and now the toads. This just has to be related to the fact that we've got that ban on spraying with DDT now."

"Why don't you tell the Smithsonian people that?"

"Oh, I wrote them. And I'm on their mailing list—for their Center for Short-Lived Phenomena. I think it's overbreeding due to overpopulation which was originally caused by the fact that we've stopped spraying and increased their food supply."

Roger pointed back at the paper. "It says that the Ozark Mountain people are very superstitious about the frogs. Like they're a bad omen or something. That's just what Marcella's been saying. Ponds teeming with tadpoles. Wouldn't you like to be down there to see it all?" Roger paused and leaned his head to one side. "Are the frogs the real reason Marcella ran away from home?"

"She won't say. She probably just didn't want anyone to know she was pregnant. But she doesn't talk about it. Not all these weeks. She's sixteen, she's pregnant, she comes from Goose Creek. That's all we know. Ma made her write a letter to her family, but no one ever answered it."

40

"We know she has a father and her friend Myrtle who reads Shakespeare."

Jo laughed. "And we know she's terrified, absolutely terrified of frogs!"

Jo's words met with a miserable wail from the piano bench in the corner of the room. "Don't you talk frogs. Why do you go on talking about me like I'm not sitting here? You always do that."

Jo laughed nervously as she spun around to face Marcella. "Didn't know you were there, that's why. If you didn't hide in corners, we'd know where you were."

Marcella pressed her hands against her rounded stomach. "When you know, you still go on like I'm not here."

Jo picked up her racket again. "Come on, Roger, or we won't get two sets in before dinner." She turned her back on Marcella and started to whistle.

"'A whistling girl and a crowing hen always come to some bad end,'" said Marcella in a satisfied tone of voice.

"Come on, Roger. Let's get out of here."

Roger shook his head. "No, let's talk to Marcella. Can't you see that she wants to talk about herself? That's why she's sitting there. Come on, Marcella, talk to us. Tell us about yourself," he urged. "What's important to you? That's what my father always asks."

"My daddy. . . ." Marcella replied, slipping off her clogs and wiggling her bare toes.

"Your daddy what?" Jo asked, thinking this might be more fun than playing tennis. She moved over on the couch next to Roger.

"Be quiet, Jo," he said. "If Marcella wants to talk to us, she will. But she doesn't have to. You just do what you want, Marcella. . . ."

"My daddy's important," Marcella said, smiling over at Roger. "He's real proud—a real proud man—and I always tried to do my best for him. And Myrtle's important. She helped out a lot after my mother went."

Jo sent Roger a secretive glance, encouraging him to probe deeper, but he was silent. Jo got up and moved closer to the piano bench. She sat on the rug and stared right up into Marcella's strawberry-marked face. "Your father and Myrtle? What about the rest of your family? Where did your mother go?"

"She's dead. Six years. There ain't no one else."

"No one?" Roger questioned gently.

Marcella bent one leg and started cleaning the lint from between her toes. Oh, my sister. . . ."

"Is she dead, too?"

Marcella shook her head. "No, just getting married. Anyhow, I guess nothing's really important—just that my baby comes with no mark."

Jo looked over at Roger. He did have a touch. He knew how to make Marcella talk just like he knew how to get her to do the same. Maybe Roger would lead Marcella on. Maybe now Jo could find out the one secret about the girl that really tantalized her. She knew she should wait for Roger to ask it, but she couldn't resist. "What about the father of your baby?" she asked. "Isn't *he* important to you?"

Marcella's face was blank. "Marcella's baby ain't got a father," she said quietly.

"Oh, come on, Marcella," Roger said. "You don't

have to talk to us if you don't want to—but all babies have fathers."

Marcella shook her head emphatically. "Baby's got no father. Just me—her mother."

Jo turned to Roger. "Marcella probably thinks babies come from kissing," she commented, suppressing a laugh. "Or from sitting on public toilet seats."

Marcella twisted her hands nervously in the faded pink cloth of her dress. "You think I'm a stupid-head," she told Jo. "A ninny. But I ain't. Babies come from men and women sleeping together. And I ain't never slept with no man."

"Well, what about a boy?" Jo asked with a scornful smile.

"No man and no boy," Marcella said stubbornly. "This will be my baby and no one else's."

Jo looked at Roger again. Then she turned back to Marcella. "No father! Ridiculous! Every baby has a father. Or are we about to witness a miracle? How exciting! How lucky can we get?"

Jo had hardly gotten the words out of her mouth when something warm and sticky struck her in the eye.

"I spit on you," Marcella cried, hitting the piano keys with one fist. "I curse you. I hope your frogs and toads give you warts, you hear?"

Then, without another word, she rose and stamped out of the room, leaving her clogs pigeon-toed under the piano bench.

Chapter 6

ROGER LAUGHED as Jo wiped her eye. But Jo was not laughing. "Horrible! Disgusting! That disgusting girl. Who spits? People don't spit. Apes spit—like at the zoo. So why are you laughing, Roger Frey? Did anyone ever spit in your eye? Anyone?"

"No," Roger admitted, still chuckling.

"Then stop your idiotic laughing. You're always feeling so sorry for Marcella. Well, that's a sample of what it's really like around here."

Jo picked up Marcella's clogs and threw them across the living room into the hall. Then she turned back to Roger. "She meant what she said, you know. She really *believes* that her baby has no father. Just like she believes that owls' eggs will cure a hangover. She doesn't even know how she got pregnant."

"Maybe she knows but doesn't want to say."

"B.S.," Jo said.

Roger frowned and tapped one foot against the coffee table in front of the couch. "If it were you, would you want to tell? Marcella is not as bad as you think. And not as dumb either."

"That's easy for you to say. You don't have to live with her. She didn't spit on you. Stop taking her so seriously. Where's your sense of humor?"

Roger grinned. "Can you feel any warts yet?"

Jo looked down at her hands. "Ridiculous! And can you see her taking care of a baby? I may have

44

teased her a little, but she didn't have to spit. I'd like to get back at her—just once."

"How?"

Jo shrugged. "You tell me. You're the one who's always full of bright ideas."

Roger pointed at Jo's terrariums. "With the frogs, maybe," he said, thinking aloud. "Do you have something small in there that might give her just a small scare?"

"The spring peepers. I have five spring peepers in the big terrarium. And you've given me a brilliant idea. I'll take them and put them into Marcella's curler box."

Roger shook his head. "Don't do that. Forget it and let's go play tennis."

"No, no," Jo insisted, warming to the idea.

"Oh, come on, Jo," Roger moaned, letting himself fall backward into the sofa cushions. "I'm sorry I even said anything. It's a terrible idea. You're too old for a corny prank like that anyway."

Jo stood up and went over to the terrariums on the bookshelf. She slid back the screen on top of the larger one. "You can call this therapy for Marcella if you like. She needs it. We'll cure her of her pathological fear of frogs." She tapped gently on the glass. "I collected these about a week ago when Ma went walking with me at night. Near the creek at school. You should see. You just stand still until they peep. Then you turn on the flashlight and reach out and pick them off the branches. They're easy to spot, because their throat sacs look like Ping-pong balls. Here. You take two and I'll take the other three."

Roger stood up and walked over to Jo. "They are

45

so tiny and funny-looking. I don't much like frogs. They're cold-blooded. And that's your problem, Jo. You're too cold-blooded. You could probably use a little therapy yourself. The way you like frogs is almost as crazy as the way Marcella hates them. Did you ever look at it that way, huh?"

"Shut up," Jo said. But she smiled as she spoke.

Roger was still hesitant. "So why do we want to cure Marcella of her fears? You think maybe we could take her back to Goose Creek then? And you'd be rid of her? You'd like that, wouldn't you? And the best part would be going back with her so you could do some research on the frog plague at the same time. Jo, I'm ashamed of you. You really are a calculating, cold-blooded girl."

Jo peered down at the little frogs throbbing between her cupped palms. "I can hold all five if you'll distract Marcella. Talk to her in the kitchen or something. And don't accuse me of dreaming up any cold-blooded schemes like returning Marcella and studying frogs. It was *your* idea. And it's crazy."

"But you'd like that," Roger said, gingerly poking the last two frogs into her hands.

"Maybe. But it's a crazy idea."

"Just adventurous," Roger insisted.

"Five spring peepers in the curler box. That's about how adventurous I feel today—and no more. What did I get when I tried to be adventurous like you? Possum meat!"

After Jo put the peepers into Marcella's curler box, she and Roger abandoned all plans for a tennis game that afternoon. It looked like it was going to rain, and Jo insisted that she wanted to be home when Marcella opened the box. That would be very soon. Marcella always combed her hair while Grampa was out walking.

Roger sat at the piano. He played some Russian dance music on the piano while Jo thumbed through a paperback novel. "You said you dance. Why don't you try dancing to my music?"

But Jo just shook her head. She wasn't interested in performing for him. After a few minutes, she put down her book and reread the latest newspaper account of the frog problems near Danville. It would be fascinating to have a chance to look at the frogs and toads herself. She *was* very curious about them.

Then an unearthly screaming echoed through the Massie house. But the screaming didn't stop. It went on and on in a series of high-pitched blasts.

For a moment, Jo just stood there listening. Then she bolted for the back bedroom. Roger was right at her heels. They got there just in time to see Marcella falling backward. There was a hollow, bumping noise, and then she lay crumpled on the floor. It had all happened so rapidly that Jo was stunned. One moment, she saw Marcella standing screaming, and the next, she was down on the floor in a rounded heap with her bony legs sticking out.

Marcella's face was drained of its normal color. Blood was running from her forehead, and some small, frightened, brownish frogs no bigger than a thumbnail were hopping around.

"Roger, do something," Jo gasped. "Catch the frogs! Do something."

"Catch the frogs?" Roger asked incredulously.

"Forget the frogs. It's Marcella we've got to worry about. *You* do something. You're the one who knows something about medicine. Get a towel. Stop the bleeding."

Jo stood there dazed. She knew she should move quickly, but she felt lost. Where was her mother? The situation seemed to be all out of control. Why was Marcella lying on the floor like that? Why was she spilling blood all over Jo's pale-green carpet?

"It was your idea, Roger," she cried. "Why did I listen to you?"

"A towel," Roger yelled, kneeling down next to the motionless girl. "Do you hear me?"

"Ask Marcella. Marcella!" Jo shouted. "Now, you get up from there. Do you hear me?"

"Jo, damn it, a towel. I can't keep holding the wound with my fingers."

Mechanically, Jo walked to the bathroom and came back with a towel. "I got Marcella's. It's clean, because she never uses it." Then, as she knelt down beside the inert body, she could feel herself gagging. "The blood," she murmured. "I don't feel too well. And the way she smells. Why can't I get her to use that deodorant?"

"Jo," Roger yelled. "Pull yourself together. Do something. She's breathing okay, but we must stop the bleeding. The blood is just pouring out."

Jo looked at Marcella and made a conscious effort to bring the whole scene back into focus. She took several rapid breaths. She swallowed hard. Then she pressed the bath towel against the gaping forehead wound. "Direct pressure," she told herself mechani-

48

cally. "Get some tea bags from the shelf over the stove. Tea will help stop the bleeding. And direct pressure. I read that somewhere."

Roger looked somewhat relieved. He hurried to find the tea bags. Jo kept talking. She didn't really care if Roger listened or not, but she must keep talking. "There's a rich blood supply here and the bone is so close to the surface of the skin that even a small bump will split it. Look, there's so much blood, I can't even see the birthmark."

Jo looked up and paused for a second. "Thanks for the tea bags. Now call Dr. Fried. His number is on a typed sheet taped on the wall under the phone. And collect the frogs, will you?"

"Maybe we should call an ambulance," Roger suggested as he stood poised in the doorway.

Jo shook her head. "She's all right. Her pulse doesn't seem fast or irregular. I should check the pupils of her eyes, but I forget what I'm supposed to look for." Jo was beginning to feel like herself again. It was, after all, only a little accident. Marcella would need a few stitches to repair the cut, but she'd be all right.

"But what about the baby?" Roger asked. "Maybe I should call an ambulance because of the baby."

"Dr. Fried will know—just call him. And I don't really think she's unconscious either. Marcella? Can you hear me? Answer me. You can hear me, can't you?"

Marcella didn't move.

"She's faking, Roger. I know she's come around. I saw her eyelids quiver. Marcella," Jo called, leaning down close to the girl. "Damn it. You can hear me, can't you?"

"Yes," Marcella said without opening her eyes. She pressed her hands convulsively against the rounded hill of her stomach. "I hear you. Can you hear me?"

"Yes," Jo said.

"Then . . . listen. I done left Goose Creek," she began, "on account of all them frogs. My dead mother was scared by a bullfrog when she was carrying me, and that's why my face is all marked up. And I didn't want no frogs scaring me. Can't have them scaring me so my baby's face is all marked. My daddy, he kept talking on the plague until I left. 'Stay in the house,' he told me, 'away from them frogs. Don't be showing your face around.' My daddy said Myrtle told him the frogs was a plague on all our houses. He said. . . ."

Jo leaned her head to one side. "A plague on all your houses? I've heard that before. That must be from Shakespeare, too."

Marcella opened her eyes. "Don't care where it's from, but if this baby in here comes out with marks on her face, I'll kill you, Jo Massie. It was Roger's idea about them frogs. His kind of idea—I know that. But you was the one that did it. And if my baby has marks on her, I'll kill you." Then Marcella closed her eyes again.

Jo shivered. She wasn't superstitious. The frogs couldn't hurt anything. Marcella's baby wouldn't be born with a strawberry-colored mark because of any frogs. This was all nonsense. She looked up at Roger, who had slipped back into the room. "It wasn't a

50

very funny joke," she admitted ruefully. "You hold the towel against her head and I'll collect the frogs."

It was all very peculiar. The frogs were chewing on the ends of the Maypole streamers, and Jo was just lying there watching them. Something was wrong. There should have been girls in long white dresses holding the ends of the streamers—not frogs. That was the Maypole, the Ladue Hall Maypole she was looking at. The Maypole she and her classmates were practicing for. How did the frogs get there?

Now the frogs were hopping to an English country tune, faster and faster. Weaving in and out with the streamers. Jo sat up. She wanted to shout at them to stop, but she couldn't seem to find her voice.

Then, before her eyes, the Maypole turned into two poles. Two skinny poles surrounded by pastel-striped streamers. Jo rubbed at her eyes. This was wrong. All wrong. And now the Maypoles were talking to her.

"I can't sleep. I'm going to look for some of them leftover beans."

Jo blinked. That was Marcella she was looking at. Marcella in a striped nightgown with her beanpole legs sticking out underneath. And a large white bandage on her forehead.

Now it all came back. Marcella's bleeding head, the trip to the hospital, her mother's anger. Marcella would be fine. She needed eight stitches and rest, Dr. Fried said. And a lot more kindness and understanding, Ma had told Jo angrily.

Then, after the hospital visit, Jo had been quiet,

51

subdued. She'd helped Ma give Marcella a sponge bath and put her to bed. Helped scrub the blood from the green carpet. And she had promised to keep an eye on Marcella. Keep her from getting up if it wasn't necessary. Now it was 3 A.M. and Marcella was walking through the middle of the room on her way to the kitchen.

"Can I get you something?" Jo asked, remembering her promise. "Do you need some help?"

"No," Marcella said. "Because of you, I ain't slept good all night. Been laying with my head aching trying to figure out what I'm doing in this place. So just leave me alone, you hear? Your kind of help I don't need."

Jo sank back on her pillow. She had tried, but Marcella didn't want her. She didn't care about Marcella anyway. In fact it annoyed her, as she realized that the girl was beginning to take over her dreams, too. Everywhere. There was no privacy.

Chapter 7

ᢒᢒᢒ IT WAS A COOL AFTERNOON in mid-April. Despite the dark clouds bunched overhead, Maypole practice at Ladue Hall proceeded on schedule.

All during practice, Jo tried to ignore the fact that Roger was sitting in the outdoor amphitheater. Except for him and Mrs. McLeod, the dance teacher, the theater was empty. Jo couldn't imagine what he was doing there. They had made no plans to play tennis. She was sure he had no interest in watching the girls of Ladue Hall go through their rehearsal.

"Isn't that Chris Frey's little brother—the one you've been playing tennis with?" Ellen Leland asked as the two of them led the sophomore class into its daisy-chain dance.

Jo glanced up from the braided rags that formed the practice chain. "Yes, that's Roger."

"What's he doing here?"

"I don't know."

Mrs. McLeod lifted her megaphone. "No talking, girls! I expect your full attention."

Practice seemed to go on and on. Although Jo loved to dance, she felt impatient—curious to know what Roger was doing there.

At last Mrs. McLeod dismissed the girls. "Only four more weeks to shape up this program," she complained. "May twelfth is our date this year. May the twelfth. You girls looked more like hedgehogs than

53

wood fairies today! Try to move with grace. And try to act like you're enjoying yourselves."

Jo turned away from Mrs. McLeod and looked up to find Roger. He was jumping from bench to bench to bring himself down to the grass, where she stood with a group of her classmates. His hands were in his pockets as he came up to them.

"Hi," Jo said. "This is Roger Frey. This is Ellen, Roz, Ellie, Susie, and Kendall."

"Aren't you starting rather young?" Kendall asked Roger. Then she turned back to the other girls. "If he's such a ladies' man at thirteen, just think what he'll be like when he grows bigger."

"Like Chris?" Roz suggested.

"Well, he's not bad-looking," Susie said.

Jo shrugged off their comments. She tried to see how Roger was reacting, but it was hard to tell. He was just grinning in his usual noncommittal way. He was shifting his weight from foot to foot as if deciding what to do. Then, after a moment, he spoke. "I enjoyed seeing all you hedgehogs out there," he said, addressing the group at large. "It's comforting to know that Ladue Hall is preparing you to assume a responsible, relevant role in life. Maypole dancing should be a very important part of everyone's education, don't you think?" Then he turned to Jo. "Come on. Let's get out of here."

Jo was smiling smugly as she and Roger strode away. True, he almost had to skip to keep up with her long-legged gait. But she was proud that he'd managed to poke fun at the other girls—to put them down.

"I meant it," Roger confided as they walked on.

"Meant what?"

"The part about relevance. What could be more irrelevant than a Maypole?"

Jo nodded. "You're right, I suppose. It may be irrelevant, but I still like it."

"Don't you get bored with a school like Ladue Hall? Don't you think all-female education is outmoded and useless?"

Jo stopped walking and looked down at Roger. "No, I don't. I'm interested in education—not a lot of coeducational socializing. Now, tell me why you came here."

"To bring a letter," Roger said as they crossed the bridge that spanned the creek separating the amphitheater from the rest of the campus. "To Marcella."

Jo opened her eyes wide. "Marcella? Was she at practice again? I didn't see her. She won't ever go walking with Grampa, but she can drag herself all the way over here to watch our practice. It's embarrassing to have that girl just hanging around. Why does she come?"

"She likes it. She doesn't think you look like a bunch of hedgehogs. She must find it very beautiful —all the fresh-faced girls dancing in the grass—all those Ladue Hall virgins twirling around the Maypole."

Jo laughed. "Oh, you're right. That's it and it just touches my heart to have our own pregnant virgin coming to see her virgin sisters dance . . ." In the middle of her extravagant metaphor, she stopped.

"Did you say a letter? Marcella—our Marcella—got a letter?"

Roger grinned and nodded vigorously. "Well, it sure took you long enough to react."

Jo shrugged. "Oh, come on. It's probably just from the Sisters of Hope. Something about her hospital room. After all, the baby's due in six weeks. Or something about a job."

"I doubt it," Roger said. "The postmark said 'Goose Creek.' Say, where are you taking me? This isn't the way back to your place."

"Up to the science building," Jo answered. "Mr. Bassett is waiting for me. Well, did you open it?"

Roger took an extra hop to keep up with Jo. "No, I would never do a thing like that. At least not without you."

"Well, who was it from?" Jo asked. "Her father? Her boyfriend?"

"It didn't say on the envelope and Marcella didn't say either. She just grabbed it from me and went off without opening it. So I stayed for the rest of your practice, because I thought you'd want to know. Now, come on. Let's hurry to your place and see what we can find out."

"Can't," Jo answered, pushing open the door to the large, red-brick building. "That will have to wait. I promised Mr. Bassett I'd meet him and his little boys to catch frogs for tomorrow's science labs."

Roger stepped into the cool, tiled hall. "Smells like disinfectant. Got to keep all the L.H. girls from getting public germs."

"Shut up, Roger."

"What is the matter with you, Jo Massie, that

you'll run after a bunch of frogs when Marcella might have gotten a letter from her lover? Aren't you curious? Just think, we could be wheedling the truth out of her right now."

Jo shook her head. "It wouldn't help if I did rush back to quiz her. She won't tell me anything. After that accident, she hates me. She even said she might kill me, remember?"

Roger nodded. "Well, then, I have another idea."

"What?"

"I'll hunt frogs with you. Quickly. Then we can hurry back to your place and see what we can find out. Okay?"

Jo smiled. "Sure. Okay."

The frog hunt was a fiasco right from the beginning. Jo tried to teach Mr. Bassett's two little sons how to poise and then pounce at a waiting frog, but Roger had other ideas. He was going to get the boys to run and chase the frogs into a bucket, so he wouldn't have to pick up the cold, wet creatures in his bare hands. There were plenty of frogs around. But the combined shrieking and thrashing of the children and Roger made it impossible to achieve anything.

One boy managed to get hold of a tiny one, but it was much too small for laboratory dissection. Jo tried to establish herself a short distance from all the commotion and get down to business. She wanted to catch the frogs without muddying her school jumper. But it was a losing battle. She got slimy when she had to pull a child out of a sewer tunnel into which he had strayed. He had already forgotten about the frog chase in an effort to lure crayfish.

Jo looked down at her spattered school uniform. They had caught only two frogs big enough to use. She was annoyed with Roger for stirring up the children and annoyed with Mr. Bassett, who didn't seem to care about the frogs at all. He was obviously too enchanted with his wet, muddy boys to remember that the purpose of the expedition had been to collect laboratory specimens.

And it was starting to rain. Jo grabbed for one last frog, who thought he was hiding unseen under a half-submerged log. Then she climbed up the bank away from the water. "I'm going," she announced. "This is crazy. I'll come back with Ma tonight, if I have to, and catch enough. But no more of this."

Leaving Mr. Bassett, Roger, and the shrieking boys, Jo grabbed her shoes and knee socks and started scrambling up the hill toward her subdivision.

"Hey, wait up, will you?" Roger called out, trying to catch up with her. "Why are you mad at me? What did I do?"

"Everything! We'd have finished with the job and been home long ago if you hadn't stirred up those children. You and your original ideas!"

"But how are we going to find out what was in Marcella's letter?"

Jo looked back over her shoulder. "You're the one with all the bright ideas. You'll just have to figure it out yourself!"

Chapter 8

MARCELLA WAS SITTING on the living-room couch cracking walnuts when they came in. The TV set was turned on, but the sound was not audible. Marcella sat in front of the flickering black and white images of some old movie, chomping on the walnuts. "Ssh!" she said, her mouth bulging with nuts.

"Chew with your mouth closed," Jo muttered.

"Ssh," Marcella repeated. "Grampa's sleeping in the next room."

"Okay," Roger whispered, leaving his muddy sneakers in the front hall. He came in and sat down next to Marcella. He cracked a nut for himself and ate it. Then he spoke. "Say, Marcella, who wrote you the letter?"

"Nobody," she said, without taking her eyes off the silent TV set.

Jo was still back in the hall. But even from where she stood, she could still see the shiny scar on Marcella's forehead. That girl's face was so unattractive, Jo decided, that one more mark didn't make much difference.

Roger wasn't having any luck with Marcella. Her lips were pursed and she kept shaking her head to all his questions. Jo wasn't going to stand there waiting, because it was apparent that she wasn't going to miss anything. She might as well go change.

Back in the room she shared with Marcella, she threw off her muddy clothes. Then she went into the adjoining bathroom to wash up. Streaks of mud ran across the sink. Jo couldn't help wondering what was in that letter. Could Marcella read? Jo wasn't even sure. She had never bothered to find out. The girl took terrible telephone messages. That much Jo knew.

She dried off and pulled on her flannel bathrobe. She made a face at Marcella's curler box as she paused to pick up her hairbrush.

Something about the curler box bothered her. Of course. The letter would be in the curler box. Marcella always stashed anything she considered important into that box. The letter would be right there, because Marcella wasn't smart enough to hide it anywhere else.

With only the slightest twinge of guilt, Jo flipped up the lid. She was right. It was sitting in there—a white envelope postmarked Goose Creek.

Jo didn't bother to look around to see if Marcella was coming. She put down her brush, slid the letter from the envelope, and read it. After she had shoved it back into the curler box, she leaned her head out into the hall. "Come back here, Roger. I need you for a moment."

"Shush, you!" Marcella called back in a stage whisper. "Can't you remember that Grampa's sleeping?"

"Well, I want Roger for a moment," she repeated somewhat more quietly.

Roger came trotting down the hall. "What's up?" he asked.

"Come here," Jo said, motioning him to follow her

into the bathroom, where she was intending to brush the leaves and mud from her hair.

"Well," Roger asked, "what did it say?"

Jo frowned. "What did what say?" she asked, brushing down through the long, red-blond strands of hair.

"The letter! The letter! I knew you'd read it if I stalled her long enough."

Jo looked into the mirror and shook her head at him. "Is there anything you can't plan or figure out?" She paused to make a part in her hair. "Well," she began slowly, "it was from her sister Allie. It said Allie's being married next week to someone named Pepper. Myrtle is helping Allie arrange everything. That makes one more occupation for Myrtle: she arranges weddings."

"The letter," Roger prodded. "What else did it say?"

"Oh, it just said that Daddy wants Marcella to come back. He needs her at home, Allie said, and thanks for writing. And that's all. No—wait—it said that the frogs are worse than ever—'all skittering around.'" Jo began to braid her hair. "And that's really it. I read it, but I didn't find out anything that we wanted to know. Isn't it always that way? You get excited and all curious, and then the secret is never as exciting as you might have imagined."

Roger sat down on the edge of the bathroom counter. "But you're wrong," he insisted. "You found out a lot. You learned that her sister's getting married next week and that her father wants her home. That he *needs* her. That's a lot."

"That's nothing," Jo scoffed. She reached and

61

pulled out the two side panels of the triple mirror. She could see three images of herself chiding three little olive-skinned Rogers. "It doesn't even say if her father and sister know that she's pregnant. And it doesn't give any clue about who the baby's father might be."

Roger peered into the medicine cabinet behind one of the side mirrors. "Don't you ever wonder about these razor-blade slots?" he mused. "The foundations of all our houses are filling up with dull old razor blades. When they dig out the remains of our civilization, that's one they'll never figure out. They'll think it was some superstitious religious custom to scatter blades before a house was built."

"Shut up, Roger. Aren't you disappointed about the letter?"

Roger was still craning his neck and looking into the medicine cabinet. "There's a razor in there. Do you shave your legs?"

"Come on. You're just trying to annoy me. You're thinking of something and you just won't say it."

Roger turned and tugged at a stray wisp of her hair. "Well, what did you expect to find in the letter? Did you really think it would be a passionate note from her lover saying to please come back so he could marry her?"

"Maybe," Jo admitted. "And you must have been thinking the same thing. Weren't you?"

Roger nodded. "I was. Sure I was. But, Jo, this letter is just as important."

"How?" she asked skeptically.

"I think you and I will absolutely have to take Marcella back to Goose Creek to be at her sister's

wedding to someone named Pepper. That girl—Allie
—is her only sister, and it's our duty to help out."

Jo reached out and pushed Roger off the counter.
"You're crazy," she laughed. "Marcella wouldn't go,
anyway. She's scared of the frogs. Remember all
them 'skittering frogs'? She thinks they're a plague
on all our houses, and besides—"

The rest of her sentence hung in mid-air as Marcella burst into the bathroom. "You nasty kids. Don't
you know it's nasty for boys and girls to be in a bathroom by theirselves? What are you up to, Jo? I ain't
going to have you and Roger playing around back in
the bathroom with your mama working and me here
in charge. Now get, Roger! And you in your bathrobe, Jo. Shame! That Roger. He may look little, but
he can't fool me!"

Roger stood there without moving. His face was
wearing its usual grin. Jo couldn't quite decide
whether to laugh or get angry. Instead of doing either,
she started to whistle.

Marcella was shaking one fist. She was so upset,
Jo noticed, that the unmarked side of her face was
almost as red as the strawberry-colored side. "Stop
whistling and listen to me, you hear?"

Roger shook his head. "A whistling girl and a crowing hen/Never come to any good end."

Now Marcella was flailing both arms angrily. "And
look at this mess in here, Jo. Clothes on the floor. Mud
and leaves in the sink. If you think I'm going to pick
up after you, you've got another think coming. And
you, Roger, get out like I told you. You ain't supposed to be messing around back here."

Roger backed away from Marcella. "Just think

63

about what I said, Jo," he counseled. "You've got to be adventurous." He backed up some more. "And, Marcella, be careful not to raise your arms. You wouldn't want to strangle the baby with the cord. . . ."

Jo stepped behind Marcella and grabbed at the flailing arms. She used force to pull them down next to Marcella's large stomach. "You're crazy, Roger," she called, looking around Marcella's shoulders. "It wouldn't work. Never. It would be a total disaster."

"Think about it, Jo. You're cold-blooded, aren't you? You could do a little basic research and collect enough laboratory frogs for Bassett for a whole year."

Marcella struggled to free herself from Jo's grasp. "What are you two talking about? You *were* doing nasty things back here in the bathroom. I knew it. I knew it."

Jo let go of Marcella. "It would never work," she told Roger. "Never."

"Nasty," Marcella repeated. "Nasty. . . ."

Jo shrugged. "You see, Roger," she laughed. "I told you. Marcella really *does* think that babies come from toilet seats."

Chapter 9

⋙ Jo HAD NEVER MET Roger's parents or his brother Chris. She was wondering about them as she stood in her white sweatsuit at the front door of the Freys' rambling frame house.

She had already pressed the bell. She wanted to ring again, but she didn't. It always annoyed her when Roger leaned on their bell. She'd just wait. Roger would come in a minute. She was meeting him early this Saturday morning because they were going to another tennis tournament. Roger's brother had promised to drive them to the bus station.

At last the door opened. An olive-skinned boy looking like an older version of Roger was standing there. He seemed to be about Jo's height—maybe a little shorter. That would be Chris.

Chris motioned with his head. "Yeah, come in," he said.

Jo tightened the grip on her bag and rackets. She walked right past Chris. If he wasn't going to introduce himself or say hello, she wouldn't bother, either.

Ahead, Jo caught a glimpse of Roger practicing imaginary forehand strokes in a sunny room at the back of the house. As Jo used one finger to hitch up her sweatpants, she couldn't help noticing a few things about the Frey house. It was quite different from her own, tidy home. There were bookshelves crowding the hall on either side with books lying half on and half off. On the floor, she stumbled over dirty sneakers and some old newspapers. She had to thread her way past two bicycles. There was a dark stain on the carpet—explained perhaps by some high-pitched barking from the rear.

Roger was obviously pleased to see her. "This is Jo," he said as she came through the doorway into a kind of breakfast room-den. "Here's Mom and Dad. This is Jo Massie. You met Chris. And the barking out back is Piper."

Mr. Frey was correcting a stack of bluebooks. He didn't even look up as Roger spoke.

"Hello, Jo," said a warm, low voice. The voice belonged to a solid-looking woman with slightly graying hair. She had a pretty, round face with bunches of laugh wrinkles around her eyes. She was wearing a denim skirt with a man's shirt hanging out over it. Jo liked her immediately.

"We're going to have some homemade corn muffins in a few minutes," Mrs. Frey said. "You'll join us, won't you?"

"Sure," Jo said. As she peered through the glass door of the oven, she could see the tins of yellow muffins.

"How long will it be, Mom?" Roger asked.

"Ten minutes. Go in the other room if you want. I'll call."

Roger gestured with one hand. "Come on," he said. "I'll play something for you." Following Roger, Jo made her way back through the obstacle course in the hall to a comfortable-looking living room. Chris

66

was on the sofa when they came in, but when he saw them, he got up and left.

Roger sat down at the piano. "Come," he said. "I'm going to play you a little corn-muffin music." Then, without further delay, he launched into a lugubrious Russian march.

Jo laughed as she perched on the edge of the piano bench. Roger had not brought her in here just to play corn-muffin music, whatever that was. He had something else in mind. Jo waited for him to say something. When he didn't, she spoke. "Your brother isn't too hospitable," she said, leaning closer so he could hear her voice over the volume of his music.

"No," Roger replied without looking up. "He's not much for making small talk, but I bet he looked you over to see what he thought."

Jo pushed at Roger's hands making them crash against the keys. "Dummy," she said.

Roger switched pieces. Now he played a slow, sentimental waltz tune. "One week until Allie's wedding," he half sang as he played. "You must talk to Marcella, so we can make our plans."

Jo smiled. So that was it. That was the reason Roger had brought her in here.

"Our folks won't miss us," he continued, swaying as he played. "They'll think we're at the Regional Tournament. Wouldn't you like that, Jo? To go to Goose Creek for Allie's wedding? We could find out about Marcella's lover. Maybe fix things up for her. You can do your little side study on frogs. Come on, Jo. Wouldn't you like that?"

Jo nodded. "Sure, if it weren't such a farfetched

idea. How can you play and talk at the same time?" Somehow Roger's idea, which had seemed so outlandish a few weeks ago, now seemed only mildly absurd.

"Well?" Roger asked, pausing with his hands in mid-air. "I had a dream about us going, and in my dream we all—"

"Well, let me think about it," Jo said. She was beginning to weaken, and Roger knew it. As soon as he gained any advantage, he always pressed on. That's how he won in tennis, too. And attending a wedding in a backward mountain town sounded like a wonderful, crazy adventure. So different from the normal, ordered days Jo usually spent.

Roger kept on talking. "Do you think Allie has a birthmark too? Will Myrtle quote Shakespeare to us? What about Pepper? Is that his last name or a nickname?" He was playing on her curiosity. She could see through him, but his scheme was working.

He cocked his head to one side. "You'll never find out unless we go. You'll never know if it's a frog plague or a toad plague."

Jo tossed her hair behind her shoulders. "But Marcella will never agree. She won't go back. She's too terrified of the frogs."

"Well, you'll just have to convince her. You said that you used to think frogs were good luck. Why don't you try to convince her that they're *lucky* instead of unlucky?"

"Maybe," Jo agreed. "But you should do it. You're better at convincing than I am."

"No, this time you'll have to do it. She won't listen

to me. She thinks I'm too young, too full of weird ideas."

"Maybe," Jo repeated.

"Corn muffins," Mrs. Frey called out. "Come on, everyone."

Roger didn't say any more about Marcella or Allie's wedding. He just got up and walked with Jo back to the breakfast room.

"I don't get much of a chance to cook during the week," Mrs. Frey explained, "so I like to fuss over something in the kitchen on Saturday mornings." Then using her shirttail as a pot holder, she pulled a pan of golden muffins from the oven.

Jo smiled at Roger's mother. "They smell good," she said. She could feel her mouth beginning to water.

Roger sent Jo one of his swift, secretive looks, but she couldn't tell what he was trying to say. She seated herself in one of the wicker chairs. Roger helped himself to a muffin and passed the plate along to her.

"Oh, take two, Roger," Mrs. Frey pleaded. "Come on, Jo. You take two. They'll stick with you all morning while you're playing tennis."

Jo reached for another muffin. She had already eaten at home, but she didn't want to hurt this kind woman's feelings. As she took hold of a second one, Roger swatted at her hand. She couldn't figure out what he was doing. "What's wrong?" she asked quietly as Mrs. Frey went over to turn out the second pan of muffins.

"Possum meat," Roger whispered.

"What did you say, Roger?" Mrs. Frey called out. "I keep telling you not to mumble."

Roger grinned. "I said, 'Let's eat.'" He turned away from the table. "Come on, Chris. Get your ass in here. You don't want to miss out on Mom's muffins."

Possum meat was an unmistakable warning, Jo decided. Roger's corn-muffin music had been the first clue. She was a little slow this morning. Oh, well, she only had one muffin. She could eat that without any trouble.

She tried to break the muffin in half, but it wouldn't crumble. The outside seemed to be shiny and crisp. She took her knife to slice through it. To her dismay, she found she had to press down with all her strength to cut it. Then, as the knife finally clattered against the plate, she smiled self-consciously.

Chris came in and tossed a muffin onto his plate. It landed with a dull thud. Jo had to clench her teeth together to keep from laughing. Out of the corner of her eye, she could see Roger with his napkin pressed up against his face.

"Come on, dear," Mrs. Frey urged, patting her husband between the shoulder blades, "shove your papers aside and have some muffins."

For the first time since Jo had come in, he raised his head. "Muffins again?" he said.

Mrs. Frey poured out two cups of coffee. "That's right. It's been a whole week, but you're so wrapped up in your work, you haven't noticed."

Mr. Frey pushed his bluebooks aside and stuck the pencil behind his ear. "Well, hello," he said. "Who are you?"

"Jo Massie," she said, glad to be acknowledged at

last. He and Chris were obviously not the hospitable ones in the family.

Jo began nibbling on one edge of her muffin. It smelled like corn meal all right, but it tasted more like corn-meal cement. Looking around, she noticed that no one else had begun.

Chris was rolling his muffin around the plate with the tip of his butter knife. When he saw Jo looking at him, he raised the knife and pointed it at her. "Do you take this tennis seriously, like Roger?" he asked, punctuating his question with short, jabbing motions of the knife. "I think it's all a grand waste of time. Running off every weekend. Working at it after school. It's monotonous—just batting a ball at someone dressed in white clothes. If you want exercise, get out and hike or ride a bicycle. See people, see the scenery. Do you really think tennis is worth the time you spend on it? Don't you think you have to give up too much to be good at it?"

Chris Frey had never even said hello to her, and here he was grilling her. He was only three years older; just who did he think he was? Jo delayed answering. She took a swallow of milk. Then she nodded her head. "I like tennis," she answered with quiet stubbornness. "I like it better when I'm winning than when I'm losing, but I like it."

Chris shook his head with disgust. "Roger should be spending his time studying. Working on his music. If he spent a fraction of the time at the piano that he does on the tennis courts, he could be some goddamned child prodigy. Tennis is a rich kids' sport and a waste of time for him."

Mrs. Frey looked unperturbed by the conversation.

Obviously she was accustomed to tirades like this from her elder son. "Butter, dear?" she asked her husband. "Marmalade, Roger?"

"No," Roger muttered. "Catsup."

"What did you say, Roger?"

"Nothing," Roger insisted, enjoying Jo's smothered laugh.

Chris was still pursuing the same line of conversation. "You ought to do something worthwhile."

Jo sat back. She could feel the wicker prickling through her sweatsuit. Chris sounded like Roger. They looked alike, talked alike. The big difference was in the degree of earnestness. Roger was always grinning and joking. But as far as Jo could discern, Chris Frey was utterly without humor.

"What's worthwhile?" Jo asked him.

"Studying," he said. "Working to get into college. I hope I'll be at Harvard next year. I help at the county recycling center. I hike. I do some experimental dog surgery with a friend of Dad's at the University."

Jo nodded.

"Jo's doing frog surgery with a science teacher over at Ladue Hall," Roger said. "And she's interested in medicine, like you."

Chris didn't look particularly impressed. "A passing fancy," he said disdainfully. "You'll grow up to be a housewife with three kids who spends her spare time playing tennis and registering new voters at the local supermarket."

"I doubt it," Jo said icily.

"Oh, Chris," Mrs. Frey said, "stop your arguing and eat. It's almost time to drive the kids to the bus."

Jo looked up and noticed that Mrs. Frey was having nothing but a cup of coffee.

"Aren't you eating?" Jo asked her.

"Oh, no, Jo. Not me. I'm dieting, and I can't take muffins of any kind. Especially since the cafeteria food at the hospital where I work—I'm a speech therapist, you know—is so starchy." She pointed at Mr. Frey, who had returned to his stack of bluebooks. "That's how I met my husband. He came to the clinic when I was just out of school to see if I could do anything for his hissing 's'. Someone at the University said that a lecturer shouldn't hiss and that he should try and correct it."

"Yes," Roger interrupted, "so Mom diagnosed him and told him that the only way for an adult to correct that hissing was for him to keep a pencil between his nose and upper lip at all times. So, you know what? His department gave him a mink-lined pencil."

Jo glanced over at Mr. Frey. She hadn't gotten much of a chance to tell if he hissed when he spoke. He had spoken so little and seemed quite unaware of the conversation going on around him. He had picked up a paperback book and retreated from the conversation. His muffin was cut in pieces but seemed to be largely uneaten. Now, for no particular reason, he looked up. "What time is it?" he asked.

Roger looked at the kitchen clock. "Almost time to go," he said. He looked across the table at his mother. "But I bet there's no gas in the car again."

Mrs. Frey groaned. "Oh, no, you're right. Why do I always do that?"

Chris jumped up. "I'll drive out to Spoede and get some gas while you finish."

73

"No," Mrs. Frey insisted. "You all finish eating. I'll go get the gas. It's my fault, so I'll go." She hopped up and lifted the keys from a hook by the back door. Then, with a flat-footed little jog, she headed outside.

As soon as the motor started, the rest of the Freys sprang into action. Roger stood up and grabbed at the muffins. He tossed them like tennis balls and, using a spatula in place of a racket, he served them into the sink. Chris turned on the water and the disposal. Quickly, he began grinding them up. The whole sink shook as the disposal tried to pulverize the corn muffins. Even Mr. Frey raised his head and passed a few muffins down to Roger. Jo was dumfounded.

Then, in a different, more relaxed way, Mr. Frey smiled at Jo. "Sorry," he apologized. "You must have thought we were a bunch of impolite slobs. But the Saturday muffins are a cross we all have to bear. It's the worst one we have—knock on wood. Roger should have spared you this by telling you to come later." Mr. Frey was grinning. A grin like Roger's. Jo liked him, after all.

"The muffin crisis," Roger interjected, "is only a small one compared to the big Birthday Cake Crisis. Have you ever heard of a family where everyone hopes that no one will remember a birthday? Maybe Chris is grumpy because he has a birthday coming next month. He's already worrying."

Jo frowned. "But what happens if the car isn't out of gas? How do you solve things then?"

Mr. Frey pointed at Roger. "That's his department. He's the one with all the ideas. He thinks up things. Sometimes he accidentally turns up the oven and burns them. Sometimes a pitcher of milk spills or Piper escapes from the back yard. We manage. Roger is always full of ideas!"

Jo nodded. So he was. Ideas about what to do with possum meat. Ideas about corn muffins. About Marcella. Had Jo really promised she'd speak to Marcella?

Chapter 10

GRAMPA WAS DOZING in front of the TV when Jo let herself in. His untended cigar smoldered in the ashtray, and an empty brandy glass sat on the edge of the table.

Jo dropped her rackets and bag and began to peel off her sweatsuit. She felt moody and dissatisfied with herself. Today's tournament had been a disaster. She had been humiliated—beaten 6–0, 6–0. She hadn't been able to concentrate at all. Despite what she had said to Chris Frey earlier in the day, she was beginning to think she was outgrowing her interest in competitive tennis.

She glanced at Marcella sitting patiently on the other side of the coffee table. Marcella was waiting for Grampa to wake up and take his turn at the checkerboard. Her patchwork quilt was draped across her lap—at least, it was draped across what was left of her lap. Every day, that stomach of hers seemed to protrude a little more.

Marcella wrenched her eyes away from the TV set. "You come home by yourself after dark?" she asked.

Jo shook her head. "No, Roger's brother drove us." Jo pointed at Grampa. "Why don't you wake him up and suggest that he go to bed? It's ten-thirty already."

"No, I can't," Marcella answered. "He don't sleep

good if he turns in too early. He'll come to in a minute and take his move."

Jo looked at the pregnant girl leafing through a magazine and watching TV as she waited for Grampa to wake up. Poor, ugly girl. Sixteen, pregnant, and marked for life by an unsightly red stain on her face. Instead of the usual annoyance, tonight Jo felt a kind of puzzling concern for the girl.

"Where's Ma?" Jo asked. "Out?"

"No, in her tub," Marcella replied. Jo smiled. That was her mother's cure for everything—a long soak in a hot tub. She claimed that it relaxed her and that she did her best thinking there, immobilized up to her chin in steaming water. Jo had tried it, but all she ever got was wrinkled toes.

Jo wanted to go back and chat with her mother. Her mother would know what to say to make her less depressed about herself, less depressed about tennis. But she hesitated. The idea of doing something for Marcella was appealing right now.

Jo turned to Marcella. "I'm going to make some cocoa," she said. "Do you want some?"

Marcella looked up. "You know your Grampa doesn't drink cocoa when he's into his brandy."

"Not Grampa," Jo said. "I was asking you."

"Me?"

"Yes, of course," Jo said, feeling somewhat ashamed. In the eight weeks Marcella had been with them, was this the first kind gesture? And, tonight, she wanted something. She wanted to convince Marcella to go back to Goose Creek. Maybe they were right about Jo—Roger and Ma and Grandpa—maybe she *was* curious but cold-blooded, maybe she *was* without compassion. But maybe she could change. "Yes, you, Marcella. I'll make you some cocoa. Come on into the kitchen. Grampa won't miss you."

Marcella picked up the quilt and slung it around her shoulders. Like some rotund queen in a patchwork train, she moved along behind Jo. When they got to the kitchen, she sat down on the step-stool. "What do you want?" she asked Jo.

Jo opened the refrigerator and took out a quart of milk. She got down the cocoa mix and a pan. "I've been thinking," she said, groping for an appropriate way to begin, "that maybe you and Roger and I could go back to Goose Creek for your sister's wedding. Isn't that going to be soon?"

Marcella rubbed one corner of the quilt against the unmarked side of her face. "You done read my letter," she said.

Jo set the pan on the stove and turned up the flame. "Yes," she admitted. "But you left it right on the dresser."

"*On* the dresser *in* the curler box. You had to go looking to find it."

"Well, yes," Jo agreed as she lifted herself backward onto the chopping-block table. "That wasn't nice. I know. But, Marcella, I really do want to help you. And your father wants you back. He needs you. The letter said so. Remember you said he was important to you? Don't you want to be in Goose Creek for your sister's wedding? Your only sister?"

Marcella chewed thoughtfully on one corner of the quilt. Jo stirred the cocoa, waiting for an answer. After a long pause, Marcella spoke. "I done already decided to go," she said. "And I decided on my own.

I don't need Roger Frey deciding that he and you should keep company with me. That was his thinking. I can go without you and without him. He's full of them ideas and you—you never was nice to me before right now—so why should I want you to come?"

Jo nodded. "I deserve that. I've been awful. But I'd like to make it up to you. And you can't go alone. The baby might come."

"She's not coming for another month yet."

Jo fumbled for another convincing reason. "But you'll need me. Remember the plague? I understand frogs and I can keep them away from you. Aren't you frightened to go back, because of them?"

Marcella sighed. "I can't be scared," she said. "I've got to go."

"Then let us come. Or just me, if you don't want Roger." Jo was warming to her task. "But, Marcella, you won't be scared if I'm there. I won't let any frog come near you."

"You and your frogs," Marcella said. "Most likely, you'll catch them to stuff in my bed."

"I wouldn't do that. Really I wouldn't. Besides, I think that it may be spadefoot toads they're having all the problems with and not frogs at all."

"Toads are worse," Marcella insisted. "Why, anyone knows that stepping on a toad will make you have an idiot child."

"That's superstition again, Marcella. Just silly superstition. And I do want to help you see your father and your sister." Jo poured the steaming liquid into two mugs. "Does your father know you're pregnant?" she asked. "Does your sister know?"

Marcella shook her head vehemently. The corners

79

of her mouth turned up in an unaccustomed grin. "Don't neither of them know. Won't they be surprised when I just walk on in?"

Jo cocked her eyebrow. "Some surprise. More like a shock. Can't you see, Marcella, you will need us? You just can't do it alone."

Marcella plunged one index finger into the cocoa to test it for warmth. She withdrew it quickly and sucked on it. "Well, I might be needing you. Can't help but be scared about going alone. Back with them frogs, too. I guess you could help if you keep feeling real nice like you do now."

Jo was feeling nice. "And, Marcella, you won't need to worry about the frogs. I think you're all wrong anyway. I think the frogs are a sign of good luck, not bad luck. Didn't you ever know that frogs could bring good luck?"

Jo smiled. Marcella would need them. It would be too difficult for a backwoods girl like Marcella to go without them. She conveniently forgot that the backwoods girl had managed to leave Goose Creek on her own. Roger was so resourceful, and she, Jo, was so sensible. Marcella would need them both. She sipped at her cocoa, her head swimming with visions of taking the pregnant girl back to her unsuspecting sister's wedding. Jo was intrigued to think that they might be able to find out who was really the father of Marcella's child.

"Maybe you'll see *him*, too," Jo mused aloud.

"Who?" Marcella asked.

"You know: *him*, your boyfriend—whoever it was who got you pregnant."

Marcella threw down her cup of cocoa. The mug

bounced and the hot, brown liquid shot all over the vinyl tile. "It wasn't nobody," Marcella maintained, easing down off her stool. "I done told you weeks ago. I ain't ever been slept with. It's *my* baby, you hear?" Then, slowly, she knelt to pick up the mug.

Jo heard. So, apparently, did Grampa. "Marcella, it's your move. You deserted me when I closed my eyes for a minute. Come back, and bring me another brandy if you will. It helps me sleep."

Jo grabbed a wad of paper towels. "Here," she volunteered, pulling Marcella to her feet. "Let me get down and clean it up. It's hard for you to get down that far, and Grampa wants you."

Marcella pressed her palms against her bulging stomach. She seemed to have already forgotten her outburst. "Thank you, Jo," she murmured. "You can be nice, can't you?"

"Sure, I can be nice. You'll see. Then it's all set? Roger and I will go to Goose Creek with you. And, don't worry, I promise—I won't ask you again about the baby's father. All right?"

"Well . . ."

"Not 'well,' " Jo interrupted. "Say 'yes!' "

Marcella wrinkled up her nose. "Well . . . yes, then. Okay."

"Marvelous. Great. I'll do everything—take care of all the arrangements. All you'll have to do is come along. But, Marcella . . ."

"What?"

"Don't say anything to Ma. Or Grampa. It must be a secret, you understand? Just the three of us will know. You can keep a secret, can't you?"

Marcella nodded. "I like secrets," she said.

Jo felt happy with herself as she swabbed at the floor. Roger's plan would work. They would all take the bus to Goose Creek next Saturday. They would go to the wedding and Jo would have some extra time to take a look at the frogs. She must remember to pack a notebook and pencils.

As soon as the floor was clean, Jo went back to the bathroom to see her mother.

"Enter," Caryl Massie called as Jo knocked.

She walked in, shut the door behind her, and sat down on the closed toilet seat. She peered through the frosted glass at the shadow in the enclosed tub.

"Did you win, Josie?"

"No, I lost. That Evans girl wiped me off the court."

"Too bad."

A little while earlier, Jo had been depressed over the tennis, but that had all faded into the background. Now her head was full of ideas about sneaking off to Goose Creek. She wanted to confide in her mother, but that would ruin the whole adventure. Her mother would volunteer to drive them all down. Jo could see the TV spot: "Wedding in the Ozarks." The fun would be in having the three of them go off alone. After all, she had been taking buses all over the state for two years. This trip wouldn't be too much to handle.

Her mother was speaking. Jo straightened her shoulders out of their slouch and tried to listen. Her mother was saying something about the Freys.

"What?" Jo asked.

"I said I talked to Lotte Frey. She said you had

some of her corn muffins this morning. I didn't know you liked corn muffins."

"I don't," Jo said. She smiled, remembering how the sink had vibrated when the muffins were being pulverized.

"And, Josie, Chris Frey said he thought you were pretty. Or that you would be when you got your teeth pushed back into your mouth—something like that."

Jo ran one finger over her braces. "It must have been Roger."

"No, Chris. Lotte said Chris—that it was the first time he had met you and that's what he thought."

Jo sighed. "So what?"

There was a slight splashing from the tub as Mrs. Massie readjusted her position. "When I was your age, I thought it was very exciting when someone like Chris complimented me."

"And look what it got you, Ma," Jo said. "Divorced and alone with a kid at twenty-two. Anyway I don't like Chris. He's a bore."

There was no immediate answer from within the glass stall. The water went on to heat up the tub.

"Ma?" Jo said. "Ma, I'm sorry. That was tactless. Did I hurt your feelings?"

There was a long pause. Then Mrs. Massie answered. "No, of course not," she said. "Listen, did I tell you about the Arab student who wants to stay with us for a few weeks?"

"No. Will he?"

"I don't think so. I told him about the bad time we had with the last one."

"Which one?"

"Which one, Josie? How could you forget? The one who threatened to immolate himself out by the mailbox.

"Oh, right," Jo said. "But his cigarette lighter was out of fluid. How could I have forgotten that?"

She and her mother laughed comfortably. Then her mother spoke again. "Oh, guess what? I've started looking for an apartment for Marcella to share with some other girls and their babies—after the baby is born, of course."

"That would be nice," Jo said.

"Is there anything else, dear?"

Jo stood up and looked at herself in the three-way mirror. She adjusted the side panels so she could see herself repeated over and over again to infinity. She should tell her mother about Goose Creek. But she wasn't going to. To infinity, she saw slouching reddish-haired girls with braces on their protruding teeth. Secretive reddish-haired girls.

"No, nothing else," Jo answered. "I'm going out now. I promised I'd help Marcella persuade Grampa to go to bed."

"You did what?"

"I told Marcella I'd help her."

This time there was a big splash. "Jo, are you feeling all right? Have you finally taken pity on the poor girl or are you sick?"

Jo tapped a light good night on the frosted glass. "No, I'm fine," she said. "Just fine."

84

Chapter 11

Leaving St. Louis with Marcella proved to be remarkably easy. Almost too easy. As far as their families knew, Jo and Roger were headed for a weekend at the Regional Tournament. They had their overnight cases and rackets. They were supposed to be staying in a players' dormitory. In their pockets they had bus money and extra cash totaling $47.50.

Marcella went with them on the county bus from Ladue to the downtown terminal. She had said she had a doctor's appointment at the Sisters of Hope Hospital. That wasn't a lie. She did have an appointment—but it was one she didn't intend to keep. At Jo's suggestion, Marcella had left a note for Caryl Massie telling her that she had decided to go to Goose Creek for her sister's wedding and that she would be back Sunday night. This way, Jo could be sure that her mother wouldn't launch a search for the missing girl.

It had been a frantic week at the Massie house. Roger had come by nearly every afternoon after school. Jo had been so anxious to keep Marcella from changing her mind that she had humored her about almost everything. "What's going on around here?" Grampa kept asking. But no one was willing to give him a straight answer.

85

If Caryl Massie noticed anything unusual, she kept it to herself. Jo was reasonably sure that her mother wasn't suspicious. She was involved in a series of assignments on narcotics in the junior high schools. When home, she seemed pleased that her daughter had at last begun to accept Marcella with understanding and good humor.

The three conspirators were relieved as they reached the Greyhound depot. Jo was happy to see that the legless vendor was not yet stationed by the door. That was a good sign. "Well," she said, "the hardest part is over. Goose Creek, here we come."

"That's right," said Roger. "Ready or not, here we come."

Each step of their trip had been well plotted in advance. Roger and Jo had even come dressed in tennis sweatsuits to avoid arousing suspicions at home. Now they separated and went to the rest rooms, where they changed back into old jeans and lightweight parkas. Then they stowed their tennis gear in a fifty-cent, forty-eight-hour locker. When that was done, they went to buy their tickets.

Jo was filled with an overwhelming sense of freedom and adventure. Roger seemed to feel the same way. He couldn't seem to stop talking and jumping around. "Once, I saw this old wino here sleeping on a bench, and he had this shiny button pinned to his collar," Roger said. "So I went closer and closer until I could read what the button said. . . ."

"What?" Jo asked.

"It said: KISS ME, I'M A PRINCE IN DISGUISE!"

Jo laughed and turned toward Marcella. Marcella

wasn't laughing. It wasn't that she hadn't understood the joke. She just wasn't listening. She seemed strangely subdued.

"Are you feeling all right?" Jo asked her. In the back of her mind, she couldn't help remembering how she and Marcella had met here in the same depot. "Why don't you take this dime and use the ladies' room before we board? It's a long ride, you know."

Marcella shook her head soberly. "No. Don't have to."

"Then what's wrong?"

Roger pushed in between the two girls. He looked up at each of them. "Nothing's wrong, is it, Marcella? Everything will be just fine. Your family, all your friends in Goose Creek will be so happy to see you."

"Shut up, Roger," Jo said. Then she turned back to Marcella. "You better tell me now what it is. I don't want to get all the way there and have you refuse to get off the bus or something ridiculous like that."

Marcella twisted her hands together in front of her stomach. "Well . . . well . . . I was just wishing I still had my lucky buckeye," she said. "It was here I lost it."

Jo bit down on her lower lip. She had really been rotten. Right from the beginning. Even now, she couldn't quite remember why she'd taken the buckeye or where she'd thrown it away. Only that she'd had no use for it and tossed it into some trash barrel.

"I'm scared," Marcella said. "Can't go back there with no luck. I'm going to the doctor and then I'll

87

just catch the local back to your place, Jo. Can't go back home without my buckeye."

"Quiet down, Marcella," Jo snapped, feeling her normal state of irritation returning. "Shut up so I can think. Why didn't you tell me a week ago that you couldn't go back without that stupid buckeye? I might have found another one a week ago. But what am I supposed to do now?"

Marcella rubbed at her birthmark with the back of one hand. "You see? You're going to be mean to me again. And you know what? I'm not going on no trip with you. You'll just start picking at me again. About how I eat. About not using enough of that sticky stuff under my arms."

"Roger," Jo pleaded. "Think quickly. What can we do for Marcella? She needs something lucky. Think."

Roger ran one hand through his shaggy hair. "How about . . . my lucky fisheyes? No, they're at home on my dresser. Let's see . . . how about . . . a rabbit's-foot key chain? I saw one in the vending machine in the men's room."

"Terrific," Jo said. "Did you hear that, Marcella? Roger will run right back to the men's room and buy you a lucky rabbit's-foot. That will make up for the missing buckeye, won't it?"

Marcella's face brightened. "A real rabbit's-foot?"

"Sure," Roger said, "with the toenails still in it."

Marcella was cheered by the furry rabbit's-foot Roger brought her, and Jo was relieved. But her buoyant mood had gone. Marcella was so difficult to deal with. Jo and Roger would have to coddle her like a little child.

Jo was very gentle with Marcella as they boarded the bus. Jo sat next to her and Roger sat across the aisle. They figured on a two-hour bus ride, which would bring them into Goose Creek about eleven in the morning.

As the bus rolled farther and farther from St. Louis, Jo stared out the window. The tinted glass of the bus gave everything an intense, slightly unreal quality. They were following a narrow road between rolling hills. In the Ozarks, Jo knew, no one exactly sees the mountains—just big hills. That was what Jo was looking at. The towns they went through looked like Alton, Springfield, or any other small midwestern town. When they were back in the country again, Jo would see more hills with trees and an occasional glimpse of a river or a lake.

Marcella had pulled a magazine from Jo's case. She thumbed through it, using her new rabbit's-foot like a pointer. "What do you suppose ever happened to the rest of the rabbit?" Marcella asked softly. "Poor little thing."

Jo looked over at her and tried to imagine what it would be like to be pregnant and unmarried and about to meet with your father and sister, who knew nothing about it. Her mind was a blank. She had never known her own father, and she'd never had a sister.

"Marcella, will your family mind that Roger and I have come along with you?"

"My daddy will like you."

"How do you know?"

"Because you're pretty. He only likes pretty people."

Jo glanced sideways at Marcella's marked face. "He only likes pretty people? What kind of a man is he?"

"Proud. Real proud. And handsome himself, too. You'll see."

Jo turned her head and looked out the window again. So Marcella's father was a proud man who only liked pretty people. Jo didn't like the answers that Marcella was giving to her questions. She wished she hadn't asked them.

At Danville, they met with an unexpected setback. The bus driver picked up his microphone to announce that there would be no service until evening to Pleasanton, Creel, and Goose Creek. A mud slide just before Pleasanton was blocking the road. It wouldn't be cleared until after six o'clock.

Jo's first reaction was one of panic. She liked things to go as planned, and any change upset her. She leaned across Marcella's stomach and tugged at Roger's sleeve. "What do we do now? How will we get there in time for the wedding?"

Roger looked over at Marcella. "How far is it to Goose Creek from here?"

Marcella shrugged. "I don't know. About four miles or five—seven maybe."

Roger stood up and grabbed for his suitcase. "We'll walk it, then," he said, pulling Marcella to her feet.

"Oh, Roger," Jo groaned. "That's a crazy idea. How can we walk that far? Much less Marcella? She doesn't like to walk anyway, and she's not even sure how far it is."

Roger looked over at her with a pained expression

90

on his face. "What would you like me to do, Miss Massie? Should I call you a Yellow Cab?"

Jo laughed in spite of herself.

"Come on," Roger urged. "Get on your feet."

"But we'll be too late," Jo protested. "By the time we get there the wedding will be over."

"Don't think so," Marcella said. "I expect they're going to do it at night. There's time."

Roger patted Marcella on the back. "See? We can make it. I'll pick up a road map from the Texaco station over there and we can check the distance. You can walk it, Marcella. You're not going to let a little mud slide keep you from seeing Allie get married to Pepper."

"Nope," answered Marcella, following Roger down off the bus.

"You're crazy, Roger," Jo shouted after him. "Absolutely crazy."

"You know," he said, "you've been saying that since we met."

"And it's still true," Jo said firmly. "Marcella, can you really walk that far—and in those clogs?"

"I'll try," the other girl said. "If I come this far, wild horses won't keep me from getting there. Anyhow, I've seen mud before."

Chapter 12

ARMED WITH A TEXACO ROAD MAP and forti-
fied by three Milky Way bars, Jo, Roger, and Marcella set off along county route #943 to Pleasanton
and Goose Creek. They had to walk single file because the gravel shoulder next to the two-lane road
was very narrow.

Despite the recent rains, the edge of the road was
dry and dusty in the midmorning sun. Traffic was not
heavy, but those cars that did appear went by swiftly,
leaving swirls of dust behind. The countryside, which
had seemed gentle and rolling from the Greyhound,
now seemed steep and endless.

"All this dust," Jo complained. "Will we really
find a mud slide up ahead?"

Roger looked back over one shoulder. "I'm beginning to wonder about that. Maybe the bus driver
wanted a day off to go fishing. Maybe he has a girlfriend in Danville."

In response to Roger's words, Jo managed a weak
smile. They had hardly begun their walk and she
could already feel her spirits beginning to droop. But
Roger, as usual, seemed so unconcerned. He walked
along humming and swinging his canvas case. For
some reason, he kept humming the same tune over
and over again. Finally, Jo poked him between the
shoulder blades. "Well," she demanded, "what is it?
Don't keep it all to yourself."

Roger dropped back a step. Then he started to sing:

"From here on up the hills don't get any higher.
From here on up the hills don't get any higher.
From here on up the hills don't get any higher.
The valleys get deeper and deeper."

Jo laughed and Roger paused long enough to take a short bow. "Pete Seeger," he said. "Roger, the court jester, is always glad to amuse. How are you doing, Marcella?"

"Doing okay," she replied.

Roger shook his head. "Doesn't anyone ever call you anything but 'Marcella'?" he asked. "How about a nickname? Something short and snappy—like Marcy. I went to Sunday school with a girl named Marcy."

"No one calls me Marcy," the girl said. "Just my name. Marcella."

The three walked on in silence for a while. Soon Jo spotted the first signs of a frog invasion. The swollen, muddy drainage ditches along the road were teeming with black tadpoles. There were so many of them down in the muddy, stagnant water that it looked like a foul witches' brew as they squirmed and thrashed. There were frogs, too. It wasn't easy to catch sight of them, but Jo could hear them splashing into the ditches as the three kicked at the roadside gravel.

After a while, Roger noticed them. "Look at the tadpoles down there!" he exclaimed. "What do you call them, Marcella? Polliwogs?"

Roger seemed to be testing Marcella's reaction,

trying to see if she would panic as she saw evidence of the frog plague. She looked into the ditches calmly. She seemed very resigned and phlegmatic. "No," she said. "I call them tadpoles."

Jo looked down at her feet. She watched her white sneakers grow tan with endless layers of dust. She didn't really want to look at the tadpoles. She didn't want to look out over the hills either. That only emphasized the distance yet to be walked. Despite all her tennis playing, the backs of her legs were rapidly getting tired.

But, no matter how hard she tried, she couldn't keep her eyes from straying back to the ditches. There, surrounding the tadpoles, she could see clumps of lush green algae. "Polluted," she muttered. "Even here." She could see bits and pieces of civilization soaking into the ditches, being ground into the mud. There was a candy wrapper that simply said UTTER-FING, an empty burlap sack marked HAYNES CHICK FEED, frayed rope, Budweiser beer cans, a dead robin, a dead snake, dead frogs squashed in the gravel by the road. All the bits and pieces of life in the Ozarks. It was a special kind of road map, Jo decided. Only, instead of walking from Danville to Goose Creek, they were walking from Budweiser to Marlboro and back.

It didn't take too long to reach the mud slide. Despite their earlier doubts, they found that half a hillside had indeed oozed down to cover ※943. The three had no trouble getting through, because one lane had already been cleared for traffic. As they passed by the flagman, they had to put their hands up to their ears to shut out the din being made by the bulldozers that were gouging away at the rest of the mud.

Jo felt somewhat better now that the mud slide was behind them. It was a sign that they were making progress. "How are you doing, Marcella?" she asked, looking back.

"Okay," Marcella answered stoically.

Was she really okay? Jo wondered, clopping along in those wooden clogs. Jo's feet were in sneakers and they hurt. She could feel a blister swelling up on her left heel, so Marcella must be uncomfortable, too. Just how much walking could a pregnant girl like Marcella take without having something awful happen?

Jo shook off these disquieting thoughts and looked ahead at the backs of Roger's denim-covered legs. Roger was whistling now, but Marcella hadn't complained. Apparently whistling was all right as long as it wasn't being done by a girl. Today, for some reason, Roger looked smaller than usual despite his brisk, even stride. And younger. He looked barely thirteen. And Marcella was so undependable. That left Jo in charge.

But everything seemed to be under control. Marcella was rather cheerful. She showed Jo a pale-green plant called May apple. "I used to always peep under them looking for the fairy ring," she said. A little later, she pointed out a woodpecker. "I used to put out peanut butter for the woodpeckers," she said. "And suet for the chickadees."

Toward noon, the traffic on ✕943 began to pick up. Cars seemed to be traveling faster, and closer to where the three were walking. Jo and the others were coated with dust. They were deafened by the

95

roaring of motorcycles. Jo was disappointed. It had never occurred to her that these hills would be filled with roaring cycles. Some of the cyclists shouted at them as they whizzed past.

"Hey, girlie, want a ride?"

"Hey, sweetheart, you forgot your pills."

"Get outta my way, you hear?"

Jo felt wearier and wearier. When Roger laughed at the bumper sticker on a truck which said IF YOU LOVE JESUS, HONK TWICE, Jo could hardly manage a smile.

Pleasanton was a relief. They walked into town, knowing they had come three miles. Now they would have a chance to get off the road and rest. Pleasanton seemed to be an ordinary town. Not as large as Danville. No one paid any attention to them—except for the few who turned their faces away to avoid looking at Marcella's birthmark.

Roger bought them hot dogs and orange drinks at the A&W. Then they sat down at the edge of the parking lot to eat. Jo was tired, but not too tired to notice that Marcella was trying to please her by chewing with her mouth closed.

While they were sitting there, Marcella kicked off her clogs. Her feet were rubbed raw.

Jo groaned as she looked at them. "Hey, you'd better wear my shoes and socks when we start up again. They might help you. I can try the clogs. Maybe they'll rest my blistered heel."

"Why don't you just go barefoot, Marcella?" Roger asked. "I bet you went barefoot at home in Goose Creek."

Marcella shook her head. "I didn't. Never. I wore

96

shoes, just like you. Got to work up calluses for bare-foot walking, and my daddy never did let me."

Jo felt good as she handed her dirty shoes and damp socks over to Marcella. She was being thoughtful and compassionate. It wasn't a bad feeling, either.

By Roger's calculations, they'd come three miles and had three more to go. After something to eat and drink, that didn't seem too bad. It was only one o'clock. If they walked steadily, they should make it to Goose Creek in another hour or so.

As they headed out of Pleasanton, Marcella stopped to pet a small stray dog that had followed them. "Don't," Jo said. The dog was dirty. It was barking and it had runny, pinkish eyes.

"Why not?" Marcella asked. "I always did like little creatures."

"Well, not that one," Jo insisted.

"Why not?"

"He might be carrying rabies or something like that. You're pregnant, remember? You have to be careful about germs and disease."

Marcella nodded. "I'll have my own little creature, soon."

Jo wrinkled up her forehead. "Are you all right? Are you sure?" She looked at the miserable dog that was still trotting after Marcella. "Scat," she cried, waving her hand. "Go away!"

"Don't," Marcella pleaded, reaching down to give the dog one more pat. "And stop your worrying. I can look after myself."

Chapter 13

ᗺᗺᗺ THEY WALKED ON. To pass the time, Jo read the names off the rural mailboxes: J. V. QUIGBY. FISH CLARK. THE CRAWFORDS. She was thirsty. The dust was coating everything, even the back of her throat. A film of dust blurred her eyes. Sometimes she thought she could see puddles of water on the road. The road would look like a grayish river, stretching ahead of them between green hills. But it was dry. That wet look was only a mirage.

"I'm parched," Roger said. "Aren't there supposed to be lots of springs around here?"

"We'll come to one by and by," Marcella answered.

"Even shade would help," Jo said. As she was speaking, she noticed that a group of five or six boys were bicycling down the road toward them. From this distance, it was impossible to tell their ages or sizes, but Jo felt uneasy. "Let's step down off the road," she suggested. "Under there—that drainage tunnel under the road. Let's stand under there for a few minutes."

"What's wrong?" Roger asked.

"Nothing yet," Jo said. "Just that we don't want any trouble and we could use a rest. It wouldn't hurt to get out of the sun for a few minutes."

Marcella was sullen. She didn't want to climb down under the road, but Roger helped by putting a firm hand under her elbow. In a minute or two they were standing in the tunnel. It reeked with a fetid smell. The water was trickling through. It wasn't deep enough for tadpoles, but little hopping frogs were everywhere.

Marcella stood still and watched them suspiciously from the corners of her eyes.

"Don't worry," Jo reassured her. "I won't let them touch you. And, remember, they're good luck. Not bad luck." Marcella didn't answer.

Jo looked around. Others had been down in this tunnel before them and left their marks. Roger laughed as he began reading off the messages: "Henry and Ellen. Tough it. God is alive and living in Tantara. Sallie loves Mary. Vengeance is mine saith the Lord." Roger shook his head. "Now, if Myrtle had been down under here, we might at least have had a little Shakespeare to read."

Jo's scalp was crawling. It was creepy under there; she was worried that Marcella might panic. She did look terrified. She took little mincing steps to avoid the frogs. Then, with a sharp stone, she scratched her name on the wall in bold, uneven letters.

The frogs were making little plopping noises as they hopped through the tunnel. They were jumping on top of one another. Jumping on top of the clogs on Jo's feet. When the bicycles finally whizzed by above their heads, some stones fell into the roadside ditches, causing the frogs to hop more than ever.

"Look at them," Jo whispered to Roger. "They *are* frightening. I don't think I'll ever like frogs again."

After a few more minutes had gone by, Jo and

99

Roger agreed that it was safe to come out. Marcella was silent, but her fists were clenched and tears were making tracks down her dusty face. Like a young child, she dabbed at them with the back of one rolled-up fist. Roger looked from one girl to the other. "Some travelers the two of you are. Jo wants to hide every time she sees someone coming and Marcella is crying already. If we just keep going, we'll be there in thirty minutes. Here, Jo, I'll even carry your case for you. Then I'll have one in each hand to balance me."

Jo was feeling irritable, too. She was beginning to feel that the whole trip to Goose Creek was a mistake. "Let me see your map," she demanded.

Roger handed it to her. Jo looked. Then she looked again. Roger had made some kind of mistake. It wasn't three miles from Pleasanton to Goose Creek. It was seven! Roger had overlooked one of the little red numbers he was supposed to be adding up. It was three to Creel and another four to Goose Creek. They'd never make it.

Jo just pointed to the map and shook her head until Roger saw what she had seen. He apologized and pounded one hand against his head. "How could I have done that to us?" he asked.

Marcella sat down on the gravel and pulled off Jo's sneakers and socks. "I can't walk no more," she declared. "My baby is kicking like the devil and I can't go no more."

"We'll have to hitchhike," Roger said, drawing himself up to his full height and gazing at Jo. "Don't argue with me, because that's what we'll have to do."

Jo nodded. "All right." She didn't see any other alternative. "Have you ever done it before?"

"No," Roger said. "But there's always a first time. We've got to be adventurous, remember? And resourceful. Isn't that why you came with me? Roger the Great will get you to Goose Creek for Allie's wedding to Pepper."

Allie's wedding. The last few hours had been so wearing that Jo had almost forgotten why they were here. "Who will pick us up?" Jo asked.

"Someone," Roger replied, "with great empathy."

Jo managed a weak smile. "Well, be careful. I'll trust you to find the right car. Don't put your thumb out for just anyone."

After letting nine or ten unpromising-looking cars speed by, Roger finally flagged down a newish-looking station wagon with two men in business suits and ties.

"Where are you going?" the driver asked.

"Goose Creek," Jo said, glancing at Roger to see if he approved of these two. He nodded.

"All right," the driver said. "Get in. I got some rug samples cluttering up the back. You two get in back and we'll take the skinny redhead up with us."

Jo didn't like this arrangement, but she couldn't think what else to do. Marcella was not going to be able to walk any farther.

Jo put her canvas bag on the floor in front. She took a seat and closed the door. As soon as Roger and Marcella slammed the back door, the car pulled away. Loud country music blared from the radio. The man next to Jo had a blond mustache and he was singing along ". . . I wonder if the going up is worth the comin' down. . . ."

The men were laughing at nothing in particular. The driver liked to pull the wagon around the curves on two screeching wheels. Jo sat rigidly. She had been nervous about five boys on bicycles, but too passive to protest hitchhiking. Now she was sorry. She didn't want to be in this car with these strange men. She didn't want to see the frogs or go to Allie's wedding. She wished she was home with Ma and with Grampa.

Roger was talking amiably with the men, telling them of their walk from Danville to Pleasanton. Marcella was silent and withdrawn. She sat clutching Jo's sneakers and socks.

Jo was suffering. If there were an automobile accident, her mother would never know what happened. She didn't even have a wallet with her to identify her—not even a library card. "Are dental records computerized?" she wondered, trying to figure out how they'd identify her.

The man with the mustache seemed to be edging closer to her. The driver kept pushing harder and harder on the gas pedal. The town of Creel came and went in a blur of gas stations. Jo sat and tried to calm herself, but nothing worked. At last, she felt as though she couldn't stand it one minute longer. "Stop!" she cried out.

"Stop?" the man with the mustache laughed. "Why? We're not there yet."

"You must stop! I want to get out," she said, pressing her back against the door of the station wagon.

To her surprise, the car screeched to an abrupt halt. The two men laughed and looked at one another. "What's the matter, Red?" the driver asked her. "What are you scared of?"

"Nothing," Jo lied. "I just want to get out."

"Okay," the driver bellowed. "You two guys in the back get out." Relieved, Jo reached for the door handle. But a large, hairy hand reached out and grasped it first.

"Red stays with us for a little while," the driver said. "We want to show her we won't hurt her."

"Come on, Red," said the man with the mustache. "We'll take you to Tantara with us. Wouldn't you like that? Just a little car ride?"

Jo froze. She wanted to scream, but nothing happened. She was conscious of the faint smell of men's cologne. Conscious of the dull silence from the back seat.

Then she heard Marcella's voice. "Got a frog sticker here," the girl said grimly. "I found it on your rug pieces. You just let her get out or I'll slice right into your neck, you hear?"

Jo couldn't believe her ears. Was that really Marcella? And what was a frog sticker anyway? Whatever it was, the two men stopped laughing.

"Don't be turning your heads," Marcella cautioned. "I done used a knife before to stick a pig and I can stick you, too."

"Get out, Jo," Roger said quietly. Jo didn't turn to look at him. She just opened the door and jumped out. Then, numbly she helped Roger and Marcella out the back. As soon as the door slammed, the car's wheels spun in the gravel and it took off. Jo, Roger, and Marcella were left standing by the side of the road.

"My bag," Jo said, pointing toward the car.

"Forget it," Roger said. "I left mine, too. And yours was no good anyway. It still smelled of possum meat. At least I have the money in my jeans."

Then Jo turned and saw the long knife. "God, Marcella! Would you have used that?" she cried out.

Marcella nodded. "If I had to," she said.

"I'd like that," Roger said. "It looks like a good knife."

Marcella shook her head and threw down the six-inch blade. "Well I ain't going to give it to you," she said. "You can't give a knife to a friend. It's bad luck."

Jo closed her eyes and swallowed hard. Roger and Marcella were already discussing knives and superstitions as if nothing had happened. "Well . . . how will we make it now?" Jo asked softly.

"Easy," said Marcella. "Right up the hill and over that soybean field. That's Goose Creek. I can go that far."

Jo looked at Marcella—a round, pink balloon with bony legs sticking out under. A dusty, round, pink balloon. "Thank you," Jo said at last. "How can I say thank you?"

"Don't," said Marcella. "If you feel beholding to me, you may have to do something for me you don't want to do."

Chapter 14

ᐅᐅᐅ Jo FELT DISAPPOINTED as they came up over the hill and into the town of Goose Creek. Whatever she had expected in the way of quaintness or special charm was missing. At first glance, it was a small town like any other—like Pleasanton or Creel. There was a sign that said GOOSE CREEK WELCOMES YOU. FIRST BAPTIST CHURCH OF JESUS. There was a cafe, a motel, a movie house, a Sears catalogue store, a cleaners', a general store, and several gas stations.

"Where do we find your dad and Allie?" Roger asked.

Marcella, who had been whimpering about her blistered feet a while before, was now standing square-shouldered, her stomach thrust out in front. Only her fingers clutching the rabbit's-foot betrayed any nervousness.

The three of them walked along the street into the center of town. They went past a machine shop marked CLYDE A. ZIRKLE, PROP. Jo could see sparks jumping from a welding torch. They walked past a shuttered, empty bakery.

"That was Daddy's," Marcella said. "But it's closed."

"What does he do now?" Roger asked.

Marcella shrugged. "Keeps his garden and acts with the Chatauqua."

They walked on—past a Chevron station with a

sign that said NO GAS DUE TO MUD. They passed by a real estate office—a pink house with a white picket fence and a sign saying CONNIE DECKER. SALES AND RENTALS.

There were some people on the street and a few cars. Mostly, Jo saw women with brown paper grocery bags, dragging small, fair-haired children. A few nodded at Marcella as she walked by with Jo and Roger. Finally someone stopped to talk.

It was a tall, strong-looking woman dressed in a pink gingham not unlike Marcella's. The woman had gray hair that was braided and wound around her head. In front, as she smiled at Marcella, Jo could see one gold-capped tooth.

"'Lo, Marcella," the woman said, shaking hands with the girl. "I wasn't expecting to see you back here."

"I came for the wedding," Marcella said.

"For the wedding, huh? Well, you're a brave girl to come—with the frogs and all. They're real bad."

"I know."

"You're not planning on staying?"

Marcella shook her head. "Just for the wedding."

"Have you seen your daddy?" the woman asked.

"Not yet."

"Well, don't worry, girl. I think things will be okay. He's too excited over Allie to take much notice of you. Now promise me you won't worry. Okay?"

"Okay," Marcella said.

The woman patted her brusquely on one shoulder. "That's a girl," she said. "Stay brave and trust to your luck." Then, with a little wave, the woman turned and hurried off.

"Who was that?" Roger asked.

"Myrtle," Marcella said.

"*That* was Myrtle?" Roger asked, looking back. "Well, I would have thought she'd be more excited to see you. Or you to see her. I mean, you talk about her so much that I'd have expected her to rush up and hug you or something."

"Myrtle does things in her own way," Marcella said.

Jo frowned. "But she didn't say anything about you being pregnant. . . ."

Marcella shrugged. "Well, maybe she already knew."

As they walked on, a few others spoke to Marcella. Someone called to her from across the street. "Well look at little Marcella Fishencor!" One boy, cutting grass, even whistled. "Was it Carter Pickett?" the boy asked. "You and him was friendly."

Marcella didn't answer. She just stared straight ahead. Jo felt that most of the people on the street were whispering and laughing behind their backs, but when she tried swiveling her head around, she never caught anyone doing it. "Who was Carter Pickett?" she wondered. Could he have been the father of Marcella's baby?

Most of the people on the street just turned their heads and avoided looking at Marcella entirely. It hurt Jo to see this. Just as she had always turned away from the pencil vendor or the girl with the birthmark, these people did, too. But people knew Marcella here. This wasn't supposed to happen right in her own, tiny home town.

"We'll see Allie over to the cleaners'," Marcella

said, apparently in answer to the question Roger had asked her ten minutes before.

"What about your dad?" Roger said. "I thought you wanted to see him most."

"He can wait," Marcella said. "Anyhow, we're here and our place is clear to th' other side of town."

The girl behind the counter was chewing gum. That was the first thing Jo noticed as they opened the door at the cleaners'. Her hair was a curly, dishwater blond. She was adding figures in an account book propped on her bare knees. Her synthetic print dress was surprisingly stylish. And she was pretty— very pretty in a delicate, small-boned way.

The bell rang as they entered, but the girl didn't look up from her work.

"'Lo, Allie," Marcella said.

So that was Allie, that attractive, petite girl was Marcella's sister. Jo found it hard to believe.

"Hi," Allie said. Then she looked up. "Marcella! You came. You did! But what are you doing in Myrtle's dowdy old dress?" She asked the question, but she didn't wait for an answer. "Oh, what a day it's going to be. Pepper is really going to marry me. Do you believe that? Of course, I didn't want to be working here today, but I had to. Old man Mohun wouldn't let me off. But you came. I can't believe it. Oh, and Squee Middleman's taking over for me for a few days so me and Pepper can go up to the city. . . ."

In the middle of this torrent of speech, Allie's voice just gave out. With eyes wide open, she stared at Marcella. She jumped to her feet and pointed her finger. "My God, look at you! Look at you!" she cried, beginning to jump up and down.

Marcella's face was relaxed. A silly grin flitted across it.

"Good for you, Marcella," Jo thought. For some reason, it made her happy to see that Allie-talking was not nearly as attractive as Allie-in-repose. Jo and Roger looked at each other as the two sisters stood face to face across the counter.

"My God! Been gone three months and you come back pregnant and looking like some dirty tramp. Some dirty, hippie tramp! Why, I wouldn't've known you if it wasn't for your face."

Marcella put one hand up against her ugly, red birthmark.

"How could you do this to me?" Allie cried out, still jumping. "How could you? Can't tell me you been married three months up in the city and look like that already. Are you going to tell me a big whopper like that?"

"Nope," Marcella said.

"Nope! Nope, what?" Allie yelled, slapping her hands against the counter.

"Nope, I ain't married."

"Then, why are you here? What are you doing here? Why this day? My day? They'll laugh at me. Even Pepper will laugh. And Daddy will be just wild. Why did you come?"

Marcella shrugged. "You done told me to."

Allie kept shaking her head. "Dumb! You are so dumb. Only you would do something like this. How could you? When I wrote come, I didn't know you was pregnant and looking like that!"

"Well," Marcella said, backing up toward the door. "Now you know."

Jo could see that Roger was excited. This was what he had come for: the drama, the pathos. "You sure did it, Marcella," he exclaimed. "You were terrific. You left her speechless."

Marcella didn't seem to be listening to Roger. She just wasn't concerned with his approval. She was too preoccupied.

"What did it really mean?" Jo wondered. Allie hadn't seemed all that surprised. She hadn't even asked who the baby's father was. Like she was playing out a part someone had written for her. Silently, Jo followed Marcella and Roger. She was tired and her feet hurt.

"Come on, Marcella," Roger urged. "Let's go to your house and get it over with your father."

Marcella nodded. "That way," she said, pointing with the rabbit's-foot.

"Look, Jo," Roger said, dropping back a few steps. "Look at the sign over that store. It says ANDY ANDY. Isn't that a funny name? And look at the sign in the window: EVERYTHING FOR YOUR PICNIC BUT THE AUNTS. Is that an awful pun?"

"Awful," Jo agreed without enthusiasm.

"And the other one," Roger continued. "SPECIAL: CHARCOAL GRAY TOILET SEATS. That's for the real conservative types in Goose Creek. And it says, ANDY WILL FIX YOUR PUMP. Do you need your pump fixed, Jo?"

Jo glanced up. The signs didn't interest her, but

the store window did have a display that caught her eye: a pyramid of Band-Aid boxes.

"Let's stop for a minute," she said. "I must have some Band-Aids for my feet. And for Marcella's, too."

"Great," Roger agreed. "I always wanted to see what a real general store looked like. Maybe the Band-Aids will make you feel better. You look droopy. That hitchhiking really got to you, didn't it?"

Jo shook her head. "No, I'm fine. I just need something to put over the blisters."

"No," Marcella said.

"Yes!" Jo insisted. "My feet feel terrible, and I know yours do, too."

But Marcella still hung back. "I'm too tired. Can't you see I want to go home?"

Jo took a deep breath. "If you don't want to go in, Marcella, then you stay outside," Jo said as patiently as she could. "I won't be long."

Marcella nodded. "Okay. You go in. I'll wait here."

Chapter 15

ROGER AND JO WENT IN through the screen door while Marcella stood outside. There was no one in sight in the cluttered store, but Jo could hear that boxes were being shoved around somewhere in the back.

"Look," Roger said, popping up near her shoulder. He was wearing a child-sized engineer's cap that said GOOSE CREEK SPECIAL. Then he reached up and clapped a patchwork sunbonnet on her head. "Look at us," he said, pointing to a small vanity mirror. "Don't you think we should buy these to dress up for the big wedding? We have enough money."

Jo laughed at the idea of their coming in in jeans and these hats, but she shook her head. "Don't make fun of them," she said.

"Oh, I like this place," Roger said, pulling off the cap. "Hey, here are some sweatshirts like Marcella's that say DANVILLE. I guess Goose Creek is too small for its own sweatshirts. And over here, look at all these jars of candy sticks. Why don't we buy some of these? See, apple stick kisses, root-beer buttons, menthol eucalyptus. And see this one—chicken bones. What do you think chicken bones taste like?"

Jo just wanted to buy the Band-Aids and leave, but still this store had something—it had that elusive quaintness Jo had been looking for. She liked the haphazard combination of shoes, food, brooms, and sunbonnets. True, there was a tourist tinge to the key chains saying GOOSE CREEK and the miniature wooden outhouses with ashtrays inside. But if she avoided looking at those shelves, there was something that made the whole store look as if it were part of another century. She let her eyes roam over quilts, kegs of nails, rakes . . .

Then, next to the rakes, she saw a bin of cheap rubber-thonged beach sandals. "Look," she said. "This is what I need for my feet, Roger, and we'll need some for Marcella, too. That will really take the pressure off the blisters."

Roger nodded in agreement. "Hey, Marcella! Marcella," he called out. "Get in here and try on a pair of these sandals, will you?"

"Marcella?" a voice called. "Marcella Fishencor? Is that you out there?" Jo looked toward the back of the store and saw a young man of about twenty emerging from the back room. He was tall and broad-shouldered with a head of hair that was astonishing. It was orange. Not red-blond like Jo's but a bright red-orange. Stiff, red-orange hair.

The screen door banged. "'Lo, Pepper," Marcella said. She came in and stood just inside the door.

"Well, look at little Marcy," Pepper said. "You came back for the wedding, huh? Well, that's a good girl. You always was a good girl, and we'll be glad to have you there." In contrast to Allie's excited anger, Pepper was cheerful and unconcerned that his sister-in-law-to-be had returned to town pregnant. He wiped at his broad face with a handkerchief. "Has your daddy seen you yet?"

"Not yet."

Pepper smiled over at Jo and Roger. "Well, who are your friends, Marcy?"

"Roger Massie and Jo Frey. I mean Jo Massie and Roger Frey," she said, blushing with the unmarked side of her face.

"Well, Roger and Joe is it? Are you both boys or one of each?" he asked laughingly. "I can't tell from your names or from your hair."

"Well, I wouldn't talk," Jo said. "If this is your store, you must be 'Andy Andy,' and that's no great name either."

Pepper sat down on a high stool. He laughed. "Say now, you must be a girl-Jo—a spunky girl named Jo. I do like women with spunk. Don't I, Marcy? Well, Andy is my father's name and mine, too. When I came into the business, he said it was less fuss to just paint my name up next to his. Sims is the last name. But no one calls me anything but 'Pepper.' My mother eats a lot of peppers—the red ones. They say that's how come my hair came out this crazy color. Now, what is it you wanted? Band-Aids and thongs?"

He grinned slyly at Marcella. "How about a licorice stick, Marcy? You never did leave this place without one when you was little. Remember? Here, take one from your almost-brother."

Marcella shook her head. "No."

"Sure you want one," Pepper urged. "You never said no before. Maybe it will be a lucky licorice. You always did want to have something lucky, didn't you? Now with all them devil frogs, you need it more. Now, take one. And Jo and what's-your-name, you take some, too."

When they were back in the street with Band-Aids, licorice, and two pairs of thonged sandals, Marcella stalked ahead leaving Jo and Roger to talk. "Can you imagine," Roger exclaimed with excitement, "what a pair they'll be after they're married. Allie never stops talking. Pepper never stops laughing and talking. Who will listen?"

Marcella propped her arms around her stomach and turned around. "He don't always talk so much," she said.

"What about Allie?" Roger asked.

"She always does."

The Fishencor house was a one-story white clapboard like most of the other houses in town. It had a pink asbestos-tiled roof. Jo noticed that a string of Christmas lights was still hanging under the eaves. To get into the house, they had to walk through Marcella's father's garden. It was filled with vegetables and flowers: onions, lilies, phlox, cabbages, a whole row of squash plants. A few chickens were wandering among the plants, scratching for bugs.

If Marcella was upset about confronting her father, she hid it well. She walked through the garden, up the front steps, and opened the front door without knocking. But, before she actually stepped in, she did turn back to Roger and Jo. "You want to stay out here?" she asked. "I don't know how my daddy will be."

Roger shook his head. "No, we came to help, and we'll do it. We're coming in with you. Right, Jo?"

"Right," Jo said. But after the scene with Allie, she wasn't too sure. Somehow she was less curious than she had been before. She wasn't sure she wanted to hear any more shouting.

"Come on, Marcy," Roger said, pushing at her gently. "Swallow hard and step in."

"Don't call me that," the girl said.

"What?"

"Marcy," she said.

"But Pepper did," Roger answered defensively.

"Did he?" she asked, turning away and stepping in.

The inside of the house was dark and sparsely furnished. The blue horsehair upholstery was decorated by little crocheted circles on the arms and backs.

A small, wiry man was mopping the floor. As they came in the room, he paused to wring out the stringy white mop. Jo smelled its sourness.

The man straightened his back and thrust out his chin. Jo stared at him. Marcella was right. He *was* handsome—even with a mop. Movie-star handsome, with wavy brown hair and long sideburns. No wonder he liked to act, Jo thought, picturing him on a stage.

As she was staring, the man spoke to Marcella. "I see you're back," he said.

Marcella nodded. "This is Jo Massie and this one here is Roger Frey," she said. "This here is my father, Ben Fishencor. Roger and Jo come with me for Allie's wedding."

Ben Fishencor nodded. "It's at seven in the school

gym. They haven't redone the church since it burnt, last Halloween."

Marcella stood there waiting for her father to say something else. Jo felt her stomach tighten as she looked from one to the other. Ben Fishencor didn't say anything else; he just wrung out the mop again and began thrashing it all over the bare floor.

"Daddy," Marcella said, after an interminable silence, "I'm going to have a baby."

Her father nodded unemotionally. "Yeah, I can see that. Anyhow, Allie phoned me an hour ago. What took you so long to get here?"

"Well . . ." Marcella began, rubbing the rabbit's-foot against her cheek.

"Well what, girl? What do you want me to say? You want me to act surprised?"

Jo shivered. Ben Fishencor knew who the baby's father was, just like Allie had known. And, despite all the protests, Marcella knew, too. Only Jo and Roger were left out.

"Say something, Daddy," Marcella pleaded. "Can't you say something?"

"What do you expect, girl? You come prancing in here in that condition fixing to go to your sister's wedding. You think I'm going to let you go like that and embarrass us all? Your friends can go if they want—your pretty girlfriend and the boy. But not you. You never should of left this house. There's too much to look after around this place. But now you're back and I expect you'll stay right here. *Inside* this place. You understand?"

Ben scooped his hand down to the bottom of his

bucket. "Got a goddamned frog in here. Goddamned frogs everywhere. Bad omens."

Marcella stood there without moving. "About the baby, Daddy. Say something about the baby."

Ben Fishencor picked up the bucket with the frog still in it, and he heaved it out the door. It clattered and splashed, making the chickens cluck with distress. Ben turned around. He straightened his shoulders again and thrust out his handsome chin. "Plague of frogs," he said. "It was the goddamned frogs."

Chapter 16

〰〰〰 WHILE JO TOOK A BATH in the old-fashioned, footed tub, Marcella took her dusty jeans outside and beat them with a broom. The blisters on Jo's feet stung in the warm water, but she put up with that in order to get rid of the dirt from the long trip. She even washed her hair with soft yellow soap and managed to rinse it under the bathtub spigot.

Then, dressed back in her jeans, she sat on the porch of the Fishencor house and whispered with Roger. He had cleaned up another way: by going down the hill and swimming in a creek. Now, as they talked, Marcella was locked in the bathroom with a box of Allie's curlers. Despite Ben Fishencor's words, Marcella was still planning to attend her sister's wedding.

Ben Fishencor had had few words to say to any of them. He remained aloof and morose. When the mopping was completed, he began to scour the stove and icebox. Jo wondered why he had chosen Allie's wedding day for these chores.

Marcella was still locked in the bathroom when Allie came home, at five. Jo had been dozing on the porch. She didn't know what Roger had been doing. It was the pounding of Allie's fists, the rattling of the bathroom door, that woke her up.

"Marcella? You hear me? You get out of there now. I got to get myself all cleaned up and ready now. You don't need to look pretty. It's not *your* wedding. It's mine and I got to get all fixed up for Pepper. And listen, Marcella, Pepper says he don't care if you came back all pregnant. He just laughed and said, 'You're rubber and glue and anything you do sticks back to you.' He says come on tonight and bring your friends."

Jo looked around and found Roger sitting under a tree not far from where she was. "Shhh!" he cautioned. And the two of them strained to hear what Ben Fishencor had to say to Allie.

"She's not going," he said. "She belongs in the house."

"Come on now, Daddy. What would Mama have said? And I want her there and Pepper says it's fine with him. I'll fix her all up—give her a shawl to cover her middle and put some make-up on her to cover that mark. No one will notice. Really they won't. You can't tell her no now. Anyhow, I'm going to look so pretty, no one will even look at old Marcella, you hear?"

Allie talked on and on. Ben kept objecting, but his objections got weaker and weaker as his elder daughter pleaded with him. "I don't care and Pepper don't care, and this way she'll just get to see me— on my day. I'll just tell her to sit herself somewhere in the back where people won't be looking her over. Oh, please, Daddy. For me—for your Allie."

At last Ben gave in. "Well, okay," he said. "You're

my pretty girl, and I never could say no to you. So she can come, but tell her to stay clear of me."

Allie was excited that Jo and Roger would be coming to the wedding, too. She dimpled and chewed hard on her gum as she showed off her wedding dress. "It was my mother's and her mother's. Myrtle helped me fix it up. She had to let out the waist, though, 'cause I wasn't about to wear corsets, like they used to."

"Is there anything we can do to help?" Jo asked, as Allie hung the dress back on the edge of the closet door.

"Oh, no. Myrtle's done near everything. And Pepper's dad, Andy—he's fixed us the cutest little trailer behind the store. It's even got a wash machine and a dryer in it."

"Are you sure there's nothing to do?" Jo asked.

Allie looked over at Jo. She leaned her head to one side. "Well, maybe—just one thing. How about you changing your clothes, Jo? You could look real good out of those dungarees, you know. You're just about as tall as Marcella. Why'n't you take her party dress from the closet?"

Jo didn't want to, but Allie insisted . . . and insisted. Before Jo knew it, she found herself buttoned into a limp blue taffeta dress with a ruffle on the bottom. Jo looked into Allie's long mirror with amazement. "Why it's not even too big," she said.

"Course not," Allie answered. "Marcella was always tall but skinny. The boys called her 'Bird-Legs.' And she wasn't too bad looking . . . except, of course,

for her face. Oh, that face. Pepper says . . . ,"
she giggled, "Pepper says he can't hardly look at it
without it making him itch. Mama was scared by
a bullfrog, you know. You think Marcella's baby
will have one like it, huh?"

Allie turned away and started banging on the bathroom door again. "Now, get out, Marcella, so I can
get in. It's late and I got to fix me up and fix you
up, too. I promised Daddy I'd find a wrap and put
some make-up on you. You don't want Daddy mad,
do you? He may change his mind and say you got
to stay here."

Allie shrugged. "Daddy's always mad at her anyway," she told Jo.

Jo nodded. "I can see why Marcella ran away.
What I can't understand is why she ever wanted to
come back."

"To show off, of course. To get even."

Jo frowned. "To get even for what?"

Allie smiled. "If you want to know so bad, why'n't
you ask Marcella?"

"Because she won't tell me."

Allie laughed. "Well," she said, "I won't either."

Roger sat outside watching Ben Fishencor chop
firewood, but Jo stayed in the house. Allie flitted
around, doing a little of everything. She found a
shawl for Marcella. She put heavy, pinkish make-up
over the marked side of Marcella's face. Jo watched
Allie spreading the make-up until all that was visible
was a shadow—as though the face was just a little
dirty. Jo was fascinated but repulsed at the same
time. It was almost worse, not seeing the mark. Now
she was acutely aware of it. Her eyes kept straying

122

back to Marcella's face to try to discover where the edges of the stain had been.

After Allie was finished, Marcella sat herself down in front of the dressing-table mirror. She examined her face silently. Then, still silent, she began to brush out her wild, curly hair. She brushed and brushed, but that only made it look worse. "She might as well be using an egg beater," Jo thought.

While Marcella was still struggling with her hair, Allie slipped into the wedding dress. It had yellowed with age and Jo could see a few frayed places. At the waist, the dress still pulled a little. But Allie looked beautiful.

Marcella thought so, too. Jo could tell by the way she turned and stared. Then she looked down at her own dress—the same, faded dress she'd worn all day. Allie had searched through the house for something else, but nothing was wide enough to go around Marcella's middle.

"I don't look very nice," Marcella said.

"Don't you worry," Allie told her. "With that shawl, nobody will see the dress anyway."

Allie talked and talked. Roger came in after a while. Then he and Allie chatted. But Marcella was silent and so was Jo. She kept wondering why no more had been said about Marcella's baby.

At last, to Jo's relief, Allie insisted that Marcella go on down to the gym with Jo and Roger. "You get good seats, now. You got to go on ahead anyhow, because it'll take Marcella longer to get there like she is. And keep that wrap pulled around you like I showed you. Then maybe some folks won't notice who you are or that you're like that. And, Jo, I know a cute boy you can dance with later. He and I used to go together before me and Pepper started in. And then after, the food will be so good. Myrtle fixed it and Daddy baked us a cake like he used to when he had the bakery. It's gonna be some night. For me. And for Pepper."

"Maybe," Roger said as they walked down the road toward the school gym, "Myrtle made us some possum-meat stew—with baked squash. Maybe Ben Fishencor's cake will be like my mother's."

Jo smiled. Another day, she might have laughed, but now she couldn't. Something was all wrong. Something was going to happen. She looked down at Roger bouncing along next to her. He wasn't upset. But Jo couldn't shake off her nervousness. It was Ben Fishencor. Something about him. His scowling. His reluctance to have Marcella at the wedding.

Marcella was walking ahead. The white shawl around her shoulders gave her a soft, Madonna-like quality. It was a fringed shawl that hung in a long triangle down Marcella's back. Maybe it wasn't even a shawl, only an old, fringed tablecloth Allie had dug up for the occasion.

Marcella wore the shawl proudly, but Jo knew that she would have gone to the wedding with no shawl and no make-up on her face. She was almost defiant. Maybe in Goose Creek it wasn't unusual for a girl to be pregnant if she wasn't married. Yet, for some reason, Jo felt that Allie was right: Marcella *was* anxious to show off her pregnancy. Despite her silence, she seemed very pleased that she was about to make her pregnant appearance at Allie's wedding to Pepper.

"Don't you wish right now," Roger said, breaking into Jo's thoughts, "that you were back in the real world—where you go to school and play tennis and dance around Maypoles?"

But Jo sensed that somehow it *was* the real world, whatever that meant, that was pressing in on her now. Preoccupied, she walked on. She didn't even notice the full moon rising and the tiny frogs hopping along by the road.

Chapter 17

ONCE JO WAS INSIDE THE GYM, her fears began to subside. She found herself being caught up in the excitement of the wedding. Now she noticed the moon, which was visible through the grilled windows of the gym. She heard the beginning of the frogs' chorus swelling in the woods outside.

The gym was lit by long white candles. A length of dark-red carpet had been unrolled on the wooden floor, and there were urns of gladioli on either side of it. Roger swore that the candles and flowers had been borrowed by Myrtle from the town funeral home.

He was full of conversation. He explored under the benches with the tips of his fingers. "Hundreds of wads of chewing gum," he reported. "Just think: right now, right under us, we have the whole oral history of Goose Creek, Missouri."

Jo laughed. She was feeling more relaxed now. It was good to be away from Ben Fishencor and away from the tension in his house.

"I wonder what we'll have for dinner?" Roger asked. "Probably . . . frog legs." He looked around at the people beginning to wander in. "How many will be here? A hundred maybe? It would only take an hour or so down by the creek to collect enough to feed that many."

Jo shivered slightly. Roger's comment about the

oral history of Goose Creek had been funny, but somehow this one about frogs wasn't.

Jo looked around. She caught sight of Myrtle in a flower-sprigged muslin. On top of her huge coronet of waxy braids, she had perched a little straw hat with a bunch of fruit on it. She moved from one place to another in a brusque, purposeful way. Jo watched her as she straightened candles, rearranged flowers, greeted guests.

"There's Myrtle," Jo told Marcella.

"I see her," the girl answered.

After a while, Myrtle came over to where they were sitting. She patted Marcella on the shoulder, but she didn't say anything but "'Lo." Marcella smiled at her briefly but did not seem inclined to talk.

By now, the benches were beginning to fill up with townspeople dressed in their best summery clothes. The women, like Myrtle, were wearing hats, and the men had on coats and ties. Among these people, Jo found she felt quite comfortable in Marcella's old taffeta with her red-blond hair hanging loose on her shoulders.

She found that she was fascinated by the beautiful faces of the pale-haired children. She wondered what it was that changed all of them into dumpy, expressionless adults. Would good-looking people like Allie and Pepper fade into drabness as they became the parents of beautiful children? Maybe not. Ben Fishencor hadn't lost *his* looks.

No one was stopping to say hello to Marcella. Maybe Allie was right. With her strawberry mark covered, no one seemed to recognize her. Everyone was so accustomed to turning away from the mark that they probably didn't know what Marcella's face really looked like. Jo was sitting next to her— on the left side, next to the marked half of her face. Even without turning her head, Jo was acutely conscious of the shadowy outline. In a way, Jo was afraid to look. Maybe she, too, would fail to recognize Marcella without it.

If Marcella had been quiet before Allie, Pepper, and her father arrived at the gym, she was even more silent, once they appeared. She sat without moving as a proud-looking Ben escorted Allie to the makeshift altar, where Pepper and Reverend Lakey were waiting. Marcella was so still that Jo had to lean closer and listen to make sure she was still breathing.

Reverend Lakey read through the wedding ceremony. Pepper and Allie exchanged rings. They kissed. And Marcella watched it all without emotion. Jo was trying to look at both of the Fishencor sisters at the same time, trying to concentrate, but something else caught her attention. It was a frog, a brown frog, hopping haphazardly across the dark-red carpet.

"That's good luck for Pepper," Marcella whispered, still without moving anything other than her lips.

"What?" Jo whispered back.

"Good luck for a frog to cross the path of a bridegroom."

As the frog hopped, Reverend Lakey was having a few private words with Allie and Pepper. Allie answered him, nodding and making faces, but Pepper was silent. He just stood there holding his head at a peculiar angle.

"He's not used to wearing a tie," Roger said. "He's afraid if he moves too quickly, it'll cut off the circulation and strangle him."

"Ssh," Jo cautioned. Now she was watching Ben Fishencor. He was the only man there dressed in a tuxedo. He even had a flower in his buttonhole. As Jo was watching, he bent down and grabbed hold of the hopping frog. Just then, Roger poked her in the ribs.

"Say, Jo, you're in a trance. I thought you didn't go in for this romantic stuff."

Jo turned her face back to the wedding party. "I don't," she answered. But, still, she was taken with the image of the petite girl standing in the candlelight next to the muscular young man with the incredible hair. And nearby was the handsome older man in the black tuxedo with his shoulders straight and his chin thrust out proudly. Jo frowned as she looked at him. "What did he do with the frog?" she wondered.

After the ceremony, came the supper and dancing. Much to Roger's delight, supper was good fried chicken, and Ben Fishencor's cake was light and delicious.

"Take home a piece, Jo, and sleep on it," Allie said, handing her a second slice of cake. "It'll be good luck. And Marcella, you'd better take one, too. You could use a little luck."

Marcella took the slice of cake. She wrapped it carefully in a white paper napkin with silver wedding

129

bells on it. Then she went and sat by herself on a bench with the shawl still around her shoulders and the ninety-eight-cent thongs on her raw feet. She sat there alone, clutching her wrapped-up slice of cake. Jo saw that Ben Fishencor was sitting alone, too. He sat by the back door smoking on his pipe. But Allie was gay, and Pepper talked to everyone. He even went and sat down next to Marcella for a moment.

Jo noticed that something he said had made Marcella laugh. Jo couldn't remember ever having seen her laugh before. "How kind of Pepper," Jo thought. "No one else has tried to make her feel better. Not even Roger. Or me."

Jo wanted to keep thinking about Marcella, but she was too caught up in the celebration. There was an old fiddler named Hubbard and a square-dance caller. Roger wouldn't join in the dancing, but Jo did. After the square dances, Hubbard played some popular tunes—even some rock tunes—on his fiddle. Jo began to forget everything but the rhythm of the music. A boy named Carter took her out to dance. But there were other partners, too. The blue taffeta rustled and swung out as she turned. Her hair swirled across her face. She felt loose and beautiful. Her thongs were long since discarded and she danced barefoot across the basketball court.

She was disappointed when the music stopped for a minute so Hubbard could put more rosin on his bow.

"I thought you didn't much like boys," Roger said acidly, as he threaded his way over to where she stood.

"I don't particularly like or not like them," Jo said. "But I do like to dance. You know that."

"What about Marcella?" Roger asked.

Jo was beginning to feel annoyed. "What about her?"

"I'm worried," Roger said. "She's been so quiet, and now she's just sitting there all alone."

Jo frowned. "Well, if you're so worried, go keep her company instead of hanging around me like this."

Roger didn't move. He stood next to her, tapping one foot. Then, when the music started up again, Carter appeared at her elbow. "Come on, girl," he said. "Let's get out there again."

Jo was about to agree when someone took her by the shoulders and spun her around. "Hey, Jo," a voice said. She looked up and saw Pepper. "It's my turn," he told her. "I got to dance with all the girls at my wedding and you're next. I never danced with a redhead before. You know why? Because I'm the only one in town, that's why. So come along, Jo. Did you like my licorice?"

Jo was uneasy. Pepper was smiling warmly, but she didn't like the way his fingers were tickling her arm. "I'm not going to dance now," she said quickly. "I'm still out of breath."

"And besides," Roger piped up, "it's against her religion to dance with redheads."

Roger's joke wasn't funny at all, but, still, Pepper doubled over with laughter. "Against her religion, is it?"

Jo brushed her hair back from her face. "Why don't you ask someone else to dance?" she suggested.

Pepper laughed again and let go of her arm. His tie was loosened now and his face was perspiring. "Well, if that's the way you feel, I may be so hard up I'll have to ask old Marcy to dance."

He turned around and craned his head until he caught sight of her still sitting on the bench. "Come on, Marcy," he bawled out. "Come over here and dance a dance with your new brother."

Jo stood poised on one foot waiting to see what would happen. To her surprise, Marcella rose carefully to her feet. She dropped the shawl. Then she stood up and walked slowly over to where Pepper was standing. Hubbard was playing something slower now. Marcella put her hands up on Pepper's shoulders. In one hand, Jo could glimpse the wrapped-up slice of cake and the rabbit's-foot. Pepper put his large hands around Marcella's back.

"Well, look at that," Allie laughed coming up behind Jo. "Look at my baby sister out there dancing like that. Our mother would turn in her grave. I think it's a sight. A sight, you hear?"

It was a sight. Jo agreed. But a strangely moving one. Marcella, who usually lumbered from place to place, was graceful now despite the rotund stomach separating her from Pepper. "Funny," Jo thought, "Marcella isn't worrying now that the baby will strangle if she raises her arms above her shoulders."

Pepper looked out over the top of Marcella's head, grinning and winking broadly at Allie. This dance was a joke to him. Some kind of big joke. There he was dancing with the pink marshmallow with the toothpick legs. But Marcella wasn't laughing. She moved slowly as if in a trance. Her face above the protruding belly was solemn and impassive.

Jo looked around and realized that the other guests were silent. Roger stood next to her in silence. Even Allie had stopped talking. "What's going on?" Jo wondered. "What is about to happen?"

Then Jo realized that Ben Fishencor was moving across the gymnasium to where Marcella and Pepper were dancing. His steps were slow and deliberate. His chin was thrust out. When he was ten feet from them, he stopped and threw down his pipe. "You filthy tramp," he cried in a strained voice. "I knew who it was all along. I knew all along."

Pepper dropped his hands and stepped back from Marcella. He was still smiling. Jo noticed that some make-up from the left side of Marcella's face had smudged on his dark-green jacket.

Marcella didn't move. She stood alone on a painted red line and looked at the circle of candlelit faces. She pressed one hand against her left cheek. Splotches of strawberry color were beginning to show again. "It weren't Pepper," she said slowly. "It weren't Pepper. That's all lying. It weren't nobody. I'm going to have my baby—mine and no one else's. Ain't never had nothing all mine. But this in here, this will be mine."

It didn't take long for Allie to find her voice. "My daddy's lying. There's never been nothing between Marcella and Pepper. Why would *he* like *her?* Pepper's just nice to her. Is that some kind of crime, huh? Pepper—look at him—he's nice to everyone. Daddy's just got it in for Marcella. He always has."

"Quiet, daughter," Ben Fishencor commanded. "You never did know when to shut your mouth. Your own husband's been playing around with your little sister and you're the last to find out." He turned back to Marcella. "Slut," he said. "Now tell the truth. The truth. Before I take the fire ax from the back door and bash in your face."

While Ben was talking, Reverend Lakey had moved up between Marcella and her father. For a moment he stood there wringing his hands together nervously. Then he spoke. "Come on, child," he told Marcella. "This here looks like a gymnasium, but tonight it's God's House. You must speak the truth here. Do it, and I can give you my blessing. Don't you want to be forgiven and blessed?"

"No," Marcella said.

Jo was about to rush over and help protect Marcella, when she realized that Myrtle was standing at the girl's side. "Leave her alone," Myrtle told Reverend Lakey, nodding her head so emphatically that the shiny cherries on her hat bobbed up and down.

Then she looked down at Marcella. "Listen to me, girl. You don't have to say nothing unless you want to. Remember Shakespeare? 'We are in God's hand,' he wrote. And we are. Now, don't bother your head with all of us. If you want to say something, say it. If not, I'll just walk you on home."

Marcella shuffled her feet. Jo stared at her—at the reappearing red mark, at the swollen stomach. She watched Marcella's lips, waiting to see if they would open. At last, they did. "Well," Marcella began softly, "I'm gonna tell you something—all of you here." She paused meaningfully. "It were him," she continued, pointing her finger at her father. It were him and his fault and no one else's."

Jo gasped, but her own small sound was lost in the collective whispering of the crowd.

Marcella was still speaking, but by now she was shouting, repeating the same words over and over. "His fault. That man. My daddy. If you're looking for someone to blame, blame him. Blame him for the way he treats me. Don't blame Pepper. Blame that man."

Ben Fishencor was shaking with rage. He was reaching to grab Marcella. "I'm going to kill you, girl. You and that bastard baby, both. Plague of frogs. I knew them frogs would bring a curse," he cried out hoarsely. As he was just about to lunge forward and grab Marcella, Jo saw him fall to the floor. Something had happened. Someone had tackled him around the knees. Jo was stunned to realize that it was Roger.

The next sequence of events blurred together for Jo. Someone was yelling, "Run" and "Run, Marcella, before he kills you." Someone was tugging at her hand. Someone was swinging an ax.

And Jo was running out into the moonlit darkness in her bare feet. Marcella was running, and Roger was there too, holding onto Marcella. They were in the dark, in the hills. Running. Running for the trees, where the moonlight wouldn't give them away. The grass was full of prickles. It was wet. There was a thorn between Jo's toes. They were panting. They were crouching silently in a dense thicket of bushes with wet feet. And there in the darkness all around them was the croaking of frogs. And, under their feet everywhere, were tiny, black, hopping froglets no bigger than pennies.

Jo reached out and took hold of Marcella's arm. "Don't worry," she whispered. "I won't let any of them hurt you."

Chapter 18

≋≋≋ IN SILENCE, they crouched in the bushes. Despite the dimness, Jo could see that Marcella was clamping her jaws together to keep from crying out about the frogs. Up near the gymnasium voices were calling, but where they were hidden there was no sound but the singing of the frogs.

Then Marcella started to cry quietly. "I done stepped on frogs and toads, and I'll get warts and my baby will be dumb."

"No," Jo whispered. "The frogs are good luck. Keep telling yourself. . . ."

"Ssh!" Roger hissed.

Jo stopped whispering. Marcella stopped whimpering. Again the three waited in silence. Gradually the voices near the gym died away, but still they huddled together without talking. At last, Roger spoke. "Let's get out of here," he whispered. "We can't stay in this place all night. It's cold and wet. I'll find a pay phone—maybe at the gas station up there—and I'll call Chris. In two hours he could be down here for us."

"No," Marcella said.

"What do you mean, 'No'?" Roger asked. "Listen, your father is after us. I saw him with that fire ax. He's after us with an ax. He says he's going to kill you. And you say we shouldn't leave."

"Can't go," Marcella said, raising herself up to her knees."

"Why not?" Jo asked. "Of course we can." She could already picture them in the Frey car speeding back to St. Louis.

"Well, you go, then, and leave me be," Marcella said. "I can't go. Running before, my water broke, and now my baby's going to come. Can't stop it now."

Roger grabbed hold of Jo's arm. "What does she mean, her water broke?"

"The fluid," Jo answered. "The amniotic sac must have broken."

"Is she right? Will the baby come now?"

Jo shook herself loose from Roger's grasp and crawled to the edge of the thicket. She looked up at the moon, high overhead. "I don't know anything about it," she said at last. The frogs were assaulting all her senses. She could hear them, see them, feel them under her feet. "If Marcella says so, she probably knows."

Jo looked back through the branches at Marcella. "Are there pains? Do you feel anything?"

Marcella shook her head. "Not yet."

Roger came crawling out after Jo. He stood up and looked around. "God, these damned frogs are everywhere. It even gives me the creeps." He reached down and pulled Jo to her feet. "Look," he whispered, "Marcella can't have her baby here outside in the middle of all these frogs. We've got to find some place to stay and someone to help. Does it hurt, having a baby?"

Jo shrugged uncomfortably. "How would I know? I've never had one."

While they were talking, Marcella dragged herself out to where they were. She paused there squatting on all fours, her belly hanging down round and swollen. "We're near to the Turner place," she said peering around. "And not too far from Myrtle's summer place."

"Could we go to the Turners'?" Jo asked.

Marcella shook her head vehemently. "Old man Turner used to work at the bakery. He'd call up my daddy right off. But we could try Myrtle's. It's empty now. She don't live there 'cept in the summer, at berry picking. Mostly she stays in town with her daughter."

Jo took a deep breath in an effort to clear her head. She knew Marcella had said they couldn't leave and that the baby would be coming, but none of this seemed to have any reality to it. It had been a long day, and she was so far from the house where she had gotten out of bed that morning.

As Jo was preoccupied with these thoughts, an eerie, shrill cry pierced through the darkness. For one long moment, the frogs stopped their singing.

"A screech owl," Marcella said in a scared whisper, hugging her arms to her chest. "When the owl screeches like that, it means some child will die. . . ."

Jo shivered. She could feel her scalp tightening.

"Come on," Roger urged. "Let's cut the talk and head for Myrtle's."

Head for Myrtle's? Just what were they going to do at that cabin? Break in and make themselves at home? Then what? Then she and Roger would deliver Marcella Fishencor's baby?

"Come on," Roger said again. "Let's start walking."

His eyes were sparkling with the excitement of this wild plan. And Marcella seemed all turned inward, absorbed in the idea that the birth of the baby was imminent. She seemed to have forgotten everything else, even the frogs.

"Stop! Wait!" Jo protested. "This is crazy."

But Roger and Marcella kept walking. "Up th'-other way," Marcella counseled, pointing her finger.

"How far?" Roger asked.

"Just over that hill there and up a bit more."

Jo picked her way over the damp, slimy ground in an effort to catch up with them. "Come on, now. Stop. Roger's right. We'll phone Chris. He can drive down and have us back at the Sisters of Hope before the baby ever comes. It takes a long time for a baby to be born."

Marcella shook her head stubbornly. "I can't go now," she said.

"Remember that your father is after us—looking for us with an ax. He might find us while we're waiting for Chris. And he might try and kill us." Jo hunched her shoulders.

Roger was too caught up in the drama of the occasion to listen. "What do you want to do, Jo, deliver a baby by the side of the road, waiting for my brother to show up? Maybe there's been another mud slide or he'll get a flat tire. That was a bad suggestion I made before. Look, we'll go to Myrtle's place. Then I'll double back to town and find her.

She can deliver the baby. She's a midwife, remember?"

Jo shook her arms about to warm herself up. The blue taffeta was not much protection against the chill of a May evening. "You mean, you'll go and leave me alone with Marcella? It's still crazy." Jo turned to Marcella. "Is that what *you* want? To have your baby out in the hills someplace with only me around? What if Roger gets lost? What if he can't find Myrtle? Do you trust me? I don't know one damned thing about delivering babies."

Marcella kept on walking. "It's all right. I do. I done watched Myrtle a couple of times. Once when she midwifed Sally Zirkle."

"Super! Fantastic!" Jo cried. "Roger, listen to me, Roger. We can't do this. Not this way."

Roger didn't stop. "You're wrong, Jo," he insisted. "Right now, any plan is better than no plan. Come on. We can't stay here. Why is it you always go to pieces in a crisis? You must pull yourself together."

Jo was so furious with Roger she wanted to take him by the shoulders and shake him. He thought this was all just some kind of game—like a set of tennis. At this moment, Jo was so angry she felt like walking away and leaving them both.

But then something happened. Marcella stopped abruptly. She swayed forward and pressed her hands into the small of her back.

"What is it?" Jo asked fearfully.

Marcella didn't answer immediately. She stayed bent in the same position a few seconds longer. Then she straightened up. "It's beginning," she said with a satisfied smile. The make-up was almost all rubbed away and the birthmark next to her smiling mouth stood out like a dense shadow. "It's beginning, and before long, I'll have my baby. My own baby, with a clean, pretty face."

Neither Roger nor Jo answered Marcella. They just kept on walking along next to her. Roger kept whispering encouragement into Jo's ear. It helped. It helped to make her forget Ben Fishencor's livid face and Pepper's laugh and Allie in the old white dress.

Marcella was feeling talkative. She said that the air smelled strange—like tornado weather. She told them of the terrifying night when a meteor had fallen near Goose Creek. Only when the screech owl cried again, did she grow silent.

Once more, as they walked, Marcella stopped for a few seconds and pressed one hand against the small of her back. But she seemed so calm that, little by little, her calmness had a soothing effect. Jo began to feel better. Either that or she was just exhausted.

When they reached Myrtle's cabin, they found it unlocked. The moonlight shone dimly through the bare windows, allowing them to take a look around. It was bare and chilly. There wasn't much in it but a bed, a table, a chair, an iron stove, and some cupboards. "Better than a roadside," Jo thought. "But not too much better."

Marcella knew where to find a kerosene lamp and matches. In order to light it, she had to put down something she had been clutching in her hand—the remnants of a slice of wedding cake squashed in a soggy paper napkin. The rabbit's-foot was nowhere in sight.

Marcella lit the lamp. "Keep it turned this way," she cautioned, "so's you don't go smoking up the glass. It's the devil to clean. And there's another one in the back cupboard if you want more light."

Weird, flickering shadows danced around the bare boards. Roger went outside to find firewood for the stove. Marcella opened another cupboard to take out a pile of Myrtle's handmade quilts.

"What are all those bottles for?" Jo asked, looking in over Marcella's shoulder.

"Myrtle makes blackberry brandy and jam in the summertime. For the tourist people."

Jo smiled. "Is there anything Myrtle can't do?"

Soon the cabin was warm from the fire Roger made in the wood stove. Jo had persuaded Marcella to lie down on the bed. She was sitting in the chair. Roger had gone out to bring in more wood.

"Now what?" Jo asked.

"Now we wait," Marcella said.

"How long?"

"I can't tell. No hurrying a baby, Myrtle always says." Marcella didn't seem to be at all worried. She appeared to be quite happy knowing that the crumbled slice of wedding cake was under the pillow on the bed.

Soon Roger came back in. He dropped his load of damp wood by the stove. Then he began to warm his hands by the fire. "Well," he said cheerfully. "Look how settled we are. I guess I won't need to get Myrtle after all. She's comfortable. Aren't you, Marcella? She'll be all right. Just fine. We'll be able to take care of her ourselves. I saw my Uncle Bruce deliver a calf once on his farm in Minnesota. And I helped Piper the night she had her puppies."

Jo rocked slowly in the old oak chair, savoring its faint, comforting squeak. It seemed cozy and beautiful in Myrtle's cabin. She had managed to forget Ben Fishencor and his fury. She could only remember the dreamlike beauty of the wedding itself. Her weariness had lulled her into a sense of well-being. Marcella seemed comfortable. In fact, she appeared to be asleep as she lay there on her side with her knees drawn up against her stomach.

"Well, why not?" Jo answered. "I saw a television film once of the birth of a baby. It just slipped right out and the doctors caught it."

Roger nodded toward Marcella. "Is there anything we should do for her now? Maybe I should take her pulse. If I take hers and take yours to see if they're the same . . ."

"But they won't be," Jo interrupted, "because she's sleeping, and I think pulses are slower when you sleep. But we should do something." Jo looked down at the damp, mud-stained taffeta. "Maybe I should wash up. That would be a beginning."

"There's a pump out back," Roger suggested, "and a bucket under the sink."

"You'll have to prime it," Marcella called out.

"We thought you were sleeping."

"Just dozing off some," Marcella said, lifting her head slightly. "Pump won't pump unless you prime it by pouring water down first."

"Oh, great! And where do I get that from?" Roger asked.

"Up under the sink. Myrtle keeps capped jars . . ." Marcella stopped in the middle of her sentence. She dropped her head down to the pillow again. "Come here, Jo," she said. "Come over and rub at my back, will you?"

While Jo was rubbing Marcella's back, Roger managed to prime the pump and get some water. As soon as Marcella had relaxed and dozed off again, Jo went and rummaged through Myrtle's cupboards. There she found several clean smocks. She was pleased. She could put one of these on after she washed.

"All right," she told Roger. "You go outside so I can wash and change."

Roger laughed. "Out there in the cold just so you can change your clothes? Nothing doing. If your clothes were on fire and I ripped them off, you wouldn't care, would you?"

"No, I guess not," Jo conceded, beginning to unbutton her dress.

"Then, why be embarrassed now? I have a mother. I've seen underwear before. So what's the difference?"

Jo giggled. "Did you ever play 'Show Me Yours and I'll Show You Mine' when you were little?"

Roger let out a hoot. "Yes, yes! Only we called it 'Doctor,'" he said.

Roger's exclamation was so noisy that Marcella opened her eyes and sat up. "What are you doing, Jo?" she demanded. "You button up that dress, you hear? And Roger Frey, you get out while she changes. You nasty boy!"

"But why?" Roger laughed, already backing toward the door.

"Because I'm still oldest here and I know what's right. Now, you get out, you hear?"

Chapter 19

When Jo had washed up and changed, Roger came back into the cabin. Marcella was sleeping.

"How about a little glass of blackberry brandy?" Roger asked.

Jo shook her head. "No, we've got to keep clear heads. There are things we should be doing. I should undress Marcella and wash her up, too."

"Maybe I should put the water on to boil," Roger said.

"What water?"

"You know, like in the old movies. They always have a pot of boiling water on the stove before someone has a baby."

Jo laughed and clapped her hands together. "Beautiful! You're being just like the expectant father yourself. That's just what the water was for—to give the *father* something to do."

Jo's words hung in midair as a low moan came from the bed. Marcella was bent double again, clutching her knees to her swollen stomach.

"Are you all right?" Jo asked.

Slowly Marcella relaxed and uncurled. Then she propped herself up on one elbow. "It's getting stronger," she said. "I reckon it's really starting in now."

Jo got up and hurried over to the bed. "Then I think you should let me undress you and cover you with a quilt," she said.

Marcella shook her head and lifted herself into a sitting position. "Not yet. First I'm going to the privy," she said. "Anyhow, I can't undress in front of him."

Marcella pulled herself to her feet. Jo saw how red and raw they were from the day's walking, but Marcella didn't limp or complain. She headed for the door. Then she stopped and turned back. "Jo," she said, "take the lamp and look around the privy for frogs. I can't use it if there's frogs in there."

"I'll take the lamp," Roger offered. He and Jo followed Marcella outside. They peered into the outhouse together. Jo noticed that there was writing on the wall. The white chalk words glinted in the lamplight. She squinted.

" 'Past hope, past cure, past help,' " she read. The words made goose bumps run up and down her arms. She looked over at Roger. He was pointing wordlessly at another phrase chalked on the wall. "There are more things in heaven and earth/Than are dreamt of in your philosophy," it said.

Jo backed away, out of the tiny shack. "I would have rather found frogs," she said, "instead of Shakespeare. 'Past hope, . . . past help'—that's not very encouraging."

Roger shrugged. "Well, the other one's not so bad."

"I guess not," Jo said. "But they left out the 'Horatio' again. I'll have to tell Myrtle if I ever see her again."

Roger turned back to Marcella, who was still standing on the steps of the cabin. "Come in," he said. "It's fine. There don't seem to be many frogs up here anyway, now that we're away from the creek. We'll wait for you right on the steps. Okay?"

"You shouldn't do that," Marcella said.

"Why not?" Jo asked.

Marcella pointed up at the moon. "Sitting in the moonlight makes people go crazy," she said solemnly.

Jo laughed and shook her head. "Oh, Marcella, we're all crazy already or we wouldn't be here!"

Marcella nodded. "Maybe you're right," she agreed. Then she lumbered into the outhouse and closed the door firmly behind her.

Roger went back into the cabin and got some quilts to throw around their shoulders. And the two of them sat on the steps, huddled under the quilts, waiting for Marcella.

"Look," Roger said, "over that way, we can see the lights of the town. Do you think they're still looking for us?"

Jo looked around her at the sharp contrasts of light and shadow created by the full moon. It was beautiful but frightening. It reminded her how alone they were up in the hills.

"Look at the lightning bugs," Roger whispered. "I bet Marcella could tell us if they were good luck or bad. She was just full of it tonight, wasn't she? Tornadoes, meteors, screech owls. Maybe we should find that screech owl and take her eggs to mix up and cure the hangover we're going to have after we sample some of Myrtle's brandy."

Jo wasn't listening to him. She was looking up in the sky.

> "Star light, star bright,
> First star I see tonight.
> I wish I may, I wish I might
> Have the wish I wish tonight."

Then she closed her eyes and wished for a healthy baby for Marcella—a baby with no birthmark.

"*You* sound like *her* now," Roger said. "I thought you didn't believe in that stuff."

"I don't, but it can't hurt, can it?"

Instead of answering her, Roger came up with an unrelated comment. "You know what it should have said in the outhouse? 'Eye of newt and toe of frog.'"

Jo made a face. "Don't talk about frogs, please! It's all so distasteful."

Roger looked over at her. "Distasteful? Does that mean you're hungry? I noticed some home-canned fruit and vegetables inside."

Jo shook her head. "No, I'm not hungry and you're not either. Anyway, we'd probably get botulism."

They waited on the steps a long time, but Marcella didn't come out. From time to time, they would hear some low moans. Then Jo would jump up and call out. "Are you okay?"

Eventually the reply would come. "I'm okay."

After a while, Jo got another quilt from the cabin. She knocked and handed it in for Marcella to cover her shoulders with.

"Does it hurt a lot?" Jo asked, lingering near the door.

"Some," came the noncommittal reply.

"Well, why don't you scream if it hurts?"

"I can't," Marcella answered. "That's not my way."

So they kept waiting. "Marcella had better be careful," Roger whispered. "If she sits there too long, she may drop that baby right down the privy hole!"

Jo smiled vaguely and watched Roger's frosty breath float out into the night. "What time is it now?" she asked.

"Almost midnight. She's been in there almost an hour and a half."

Jo got up and pressed her face against the splintery boards. "Marcella," she pleaded. "Come out. Let me put you back to bed now."

"No," Marcella answered. "I feel better here. No frogs can get in, neither. I didn't like it lying down."

Jo dragged her quilt back and sat down next to Roger. "I think," she said, "as long as we're waiting all this time that we should discuss what we have to do to deliver a baby."

Roger tapped his fingers on the wooden boards of the porch. "You said in the film you saw that the doctors just caught it. That's what we did with the puppies. They came and we helped pull them out."

"Get the lantern. See if you can find a pencil and paper inside. We'll make a list. That will help."

Roger got the pencil and a brown paper bag to write on. "All right, you said no hot water. So where do we begin?"

Jo reconsidered. "Maybe a little hot water wouldn't hurt. We could make Marcella some tea if she wanted it. And we might need boiling water to sterilize a knife for cutting the umbilical cord."

"Cutting the cord!" Roger groaned. "We'll have to do that? What do we do? Tie it in a knot?"

Jo pulled the quilt tighter around her shoulders. "Maybe. Or we'll use some string. Put string on the list too, and we'll search for it when we go in."

While Marcella continued to sigh and moan from inside the outhouse, Jo and Roger worked over their list. They had decided that they didn't need diapers or diaper pins. They'd just wrap the baby in a clean towel.

"What about food for the baby?" Roger asked.

Jo smiled. "That's not our worry. Marcella comes equipped to handle that!"

Roger changed the subject. "Well, do we slap it on the bottom when it comes out?"

Jo shook her head. "They don't do that any more. Only in the same old movies with the kettles of hot water. Now they clean the nose and throat with sterile cotton swabs or something."

"Now, just where are we supposed to find cotton swabs?"

Jo nodded her head. "All right. Then we will have to plan to spank it on the bottom." She paused. "I wonder what happens with the afterbirth. Is there a lot of bleeding?"

"Uncle Bruce's cow ate the afterbirth," Roger said.

"Shut up," Jo said. She was beginning to feel uneasy again. "What will we do if there's a lot of bleeding? Maybe the baby will die or be born dead."

She could feel herself shaking now. No, it wasn't her. It was Roger shaking her.

"Stop it! Stop it," he insisted. "Don't get that way."

"Have you ever seen a dead person?" Jo asked. "Remember in *Huck Finn* when he finds that body down by the river?"

"No," Roger said. "And we're not going to see one tonight, you understand?"

"Maybe," Jo said.

"You need to look at this all from a different point of view. Do you believe in God?"

"No," Jo answered. "Yes, I mean. I don't know. What does that have to do with Marcella and her baby?"

Roger looked over at Jo. "Maybe nothing. Maybe everything," he said. "Maybe you should try praying. Maybe praying would make you feel better."

Jo laughed sardonically. Roger had a solution for everything. His solution for Jo's depression and fears of death: prayer. She'd never, never heard him mention God before.

But as Jo was laughing, the door to the outhouse creaked and Marcella appeared in the doorway. She just stood there leaning against the doorframe. Her face was drawn and haggard. It looked absolutely white—ghostly in the moonlight. It was shining with beads of perspiration despite the coolness of the air. Jo bit down on her bottom lip.

"Pray," Roger whispered to her.

"I can't," she breathed.

"Let's go inside now—me and you, Jo," Marcella said. "I'm ready to undress and lay down."

"Okay, sure," Roger agreed.

Marcella shook her head in a slow, weary way. "Not okay," she said weakly. "Not you. Just Jo. Can't have you seeing me naked. It's not nice. You got to stay out here."

Roger hurried toward Marcella. "No," he insisted. "You'll need me. Jo will need me. I must come in."

Instead of answering, Marcella fell forward to her knees and bent her head down to the ground. Jo could see that her body was gripped by a powerful contraction, but the girl didn't cry out. Only a low moan escaped. Then, after about a minute, she looked up again. "You gonna stay out, Roger," she whispered in a tight little voice, "you hear?"

"No," Roger cried. "I won't. Jo can't do it alone."

Jo straightened her own shoulders. Then she moved forward and helped Marcella to her feet. This was no longer a time of fantasies about babies or making lists on grocery bags. "Whatever you want, Marcella," Jo agreed slowly. "That's the way things will be." She turned to Roger. "You'll have to stay outside," she said gently. "We'll do it Marcella's way." Then she began leading the other girl back to the cabin.

"I'll run and see if I can find Myrtle," Roger volunteered.

Jo shook her head. "Not now. It may be too late. And you must stay here now for me." She looked down at him standing there helplessly clenching and unclenching his fists. "Stay for me. I'll be all right in there as long as I know you're right out here. But don't leave me alone."

Roger nodded. "I'll stay," he agreed. "Outside. And when you get in . . . maybe you'd better pray."

Jo didn't answer. She just reached out and wiped some of the perspiration from Marcella's forehead.

Chapter 20

As the water boiled, the old tin berry pot rattled and rocked back and forth on the iron stove. Clouds of steam rose from the pot.

Jo had come inside with Marcella expecting something—expecting that Marcella would lie down, the baby would slip out, and she, somehow, would catch it. But that never happened. Instead, Marcella lay doubled up on the bed. Every minute or so, she would stiffen and clench her teeth together. New beads of sweat would seep out onto her forehead. Jo was perspiring too. Perhaps out of nervousness. Perhaps just because the wood fire and steaming pot had made the cabin so humid.

"What's happening? What's going on?" Roger kept asking, pressing his nose against a crack in the door.

"Nothing," Jo kept answering, vaguely wishing that she, too, were outside. "Please, Marcella," she asked at last, "let me open the door a little."

"No," Marcella said. "Can't have the night air in here. Night air's full of poison."

Jo sat helplessly in the wooden rocker, gripping its splintery arms. As she sat, she found herself becoming more and more tense. She was obsessed with a desire to whistle, but she didn't. That, too, would upset Marcella.

Roger was outside saying too much, and she was inside with Marcella, who wasn't saying anything.

No matter how much she tried to control herself, she was still afraid.

Then, as Jo was sitting there rigidly, Marcella finally dragged herself up from the bed. She unbuttoned her dress. She let it drop to the floor. Unnerved, Jo stared at her—at the swollen, pregnant body of the other girl. She felt a spasm in her own stomach. Looking down, she pressed one hand against her stomach until she felt its own incredible taut flatness. Then she looked over again at Marcella's distended shape. Suddenly, she realized that she was in the wrong place at the wrong time. She was the wrong person. This was the real thing. The real world. She was too weak. She was not equipped to deal with it.

As she stared at Marcella's body, something suddenly snapped. Jo started to cry and wail and scream. She sat in the rocker, clutching her knees to her chest, sobbing uncontrollably. "I can't do it. I can't deliver any baby. I wish I was home. I wish I'd never seen any of you—not you, not Roger. Why am I here? I must be crazy. Crazy. Crazy." Her words were punctuated by gasps and choking sounds.

As she sobbed and cried out, she was dimly aware of Roger's voice. He was shouting something, but he was so busy shouting he seemed to think it was Marcella crying. Jo struggled to control herself long enough to answer him, but she couldn't. It was Marcella who shouted back at him. "Shut your mouth and leave us be," she said.

Jo was rubbing her wet face back and forth against her kneecaps when she heard the creaking floor boards. She looked up in time to see Marcella, wrapped in a quilt, coming slowly over to her. Marcella squatted down by the chair. She patted Jo on the head, on the back. "There, there," she crooned. "There, there, dear. Can't have this. You've got to be helping me, you hear? You're strong and smart. And you got to bring my baby and bring me that good luck, you hear? Come on, dear. Dry your tears."

Jo looked up through a film of tears. She rested her chin on her knees. Marcella was mothering her. Being tender and gentle, just as she would be with her own baby—the baby Jo was supposed to deliver. A real baby. "I want Roger," Jo pleaded. "I can't stay in here alone with you."

Marcella shook her head. "Can't have him in here. It's not right. It's messy business when the baby comes, he'll cry or get sick. Listen, remember how you took care of me when my head was busted open? He weren't no good then and he won't be good now."

Marcella was wrong. Jo knew that. She had gone to pieces then, just as she was doing now. She licked at the salt tears clinging to her knees. She was going to beg once more, hoping Marcella would relent and let Roger come in.

Then, out of the corner of her eye, she saw something white and bony. It was Marcella gripping the arm of the rocking chair, holding it so tightly that the bones seemed to be stripped of their flesh. Jo looked beyond the knuckles to the taut, pained face—the straining, strawberry-marked face. As Jo stared, the moment seemed endless. Then, at last, Marcella's features began to relax as the contraction eased.

Marcella took a deep breath before she spoke again. "I'm counting on you, Jo. Don't let me down."

Jo straightened up. She reached out until her hand was almost touching Marcella's. What was she going to do? Pat Marcella on the hand and tell her everything would be all right? No, Marcella needed something more than a pat on the hand. Jo drew her hand back into her own lap.

With great effort, she found her voice. "All right," she said, dropping her feet to the floor, "get yourself into bed, Marcella. I'm going to begin looking after *you*."

Marcella smiled. She obeyed. She padded back to the bed. Then she lay on her side covered by one of Myrtle's handmade quilts.

"I'm sorry, Jo, but I keep sweating," Marcella said softly. "Sweating and sweating. It must bother your nose something awful."

Jo sat down on the edge of the bed. "Don't be ridiculous," she told Marcella. "Who cares if you perspire? There's nothing wrong with the smell of good, honest sweat."

Jo began to busy herself inside the cabin. She wanted to shut her mind to everything but the immediate present. She mustn't think about her family or Marcella's. Even about the baby yet. She had regained an outer sense of calm, but deep down she was still terrified that Marcella's fears would become reality if she even thought them. Marcella would die. The baby would be born with a birthmark. Marcella would rise up and kill her because of the marked infant. Or Ben Fishencor would appear and kill them all.

159

So, to maintain the illusion of calmness, she concentrated on putting new wood in the stove, arranging a stack of clean towels, looking for string. She wiped Marcella's forehead. She rubbed her back. There was no past and no future. Just this single moment in time and space. She was aware of everything inside the cabin: the flickering light of the lantern, the rattle of the pot, the squeak of the chair.

Every once in a while, Jo would remember what Roger had said about praying. But she didn't do it. She was too busy. Marcella needed her, and the lamp was running low on kerosene. Besides, she wouldn't have known what to say.

Roger kept calling from outside the door. She was trying to ignore him, because his voice seemed to be rising to a pitch of hysteria. Marcella had been right. He did belong outside. She had all she could manage with Marcella and herself. There wasn't enough energy left over to look after a thirteen-year-old kid. After a while, she just kept blotting out his words and crying out, "Shut up. Leave us alone."

That was the reason why it took her so long to realize that Roger was yelling something about someone coming up the hill with a flashlight. She heard his voice and his words. But she was busy. Marcella was crying. Her face was contorted with pain. Jo couldn't worry about anyone but Marcella now. Whoever it was coming up that hill now would just have to keep coming. That person, whoever he might be, was not going to hurt Marcella. Jo wished she had the frog sticker Marcella had found in the men's car or the ax from the gym. She felt superhuman.

Marcella was enduring enough. Jo wasn't going to let anyone touch her.

When the cabin door flew open, Jo didn't move. Marcella was gripping her hands, digging her finger-nails into Jo's palms. That was all that mattered at that moment.

"You mean you didn't give her any brandy?" a querulous voice called out. "You some kind of damned fool or something? The whole blasted place is full of brandy and you don't even give her a sip?"

Only then did Jo look up. It was Myrtle—Myrtle herself, holding a powerful, big-beam flashlight that rid the cabin of its flickering shadows. Jo squinted at its brightness. She felt like falling to the floor and hugging Myrtle around the knees. If she'd taken the time to pray, this is what she would have prayed for—a midwife to deliver Marcella's baby.

Chapter 21

MYRTLE TOOK CHARGE IMMEDIATELY. She pulled the pot of water off the stove and opened one shutter to let some air in. Then she gave Marcella a cupful of brandy. "That'll ease the pains and slow 'em down some, give me time to get myself ready and time to check her over." Myrtle put the bottle of brandy into Jo's hands. "Here. You'd better take a shot yourself. Looks like you could use it."

Jo watched with fascination as Myrtle examined Marcella. She moved her strong hands over the girl's abdomen. Then she pressed one ear against her stomach and listened for the baby's heartbeat.

"How did you know we were up here?" Jo asked.

Myrtle snorted and readjusted some of the hairpins from her coronet of braids. "You can see town from here, can't you? Well, I could see you. I just looked out the window at Clara's and saw the cabin light. I figured you'd be here. Marcella always used to run here to hide from her daddy when he was in a temper. I wasn't fixing to come up 'til I saw that no one was about to put out the lamp."

Myrtle ran her hands lightly over Marcella's abdomen. She frowned at Jo. "What were you doing, anyway? You think you know one damned thing about bringing out a baby? I've brought quite a few in my day—and every single time it scares me shitless! Who did you expect was going to help you—God?"

162

Jo sank back in the rocker. "Maybe," she said. "Marcella always talks so much about luck. Maybe we were trusting to luck. . . ."

"Well, listen, girl," Myrtle told her. "There's good luck and bad luck, but mostly you got to make your own luck. God helps them that helps themselves. Or, like Shakespeare said, 'Nothing comes from nothing.'"

Then Myrtle turned back toward Marcella to help ease her through another contraction. As soon as the girl was comfortable again, Myrtle spoke to Jo. "Now get up and tell your long-haired little friend that he should stop banging and whimpering like *he's* the one having the baby. You just tell him he can't come in. And bolt the door when you've told him."

Slowly Jo crossed the room. She opened the door a crack and smiled wanly at Roger. "I'm sorry," she said. He nodded forlornly. Jo felt like reaching out and patting him on the head, but she didn't. She just sighed and closed the door. Then, as Myrtle had ordered, she bolted it. She would never have done that if she were alone. She had always intended to scream for Roger, to scream for him to come in and help as the baby appeared. But Myrtle was in charge now.

The only sound in the cabin was Marcella's moaning and a dry, persistent cough that kept bothering Myrtle. "Nerves," she told Jo, as a way of explaining the cough, "or asthma. I could cure it in a minute if I'd go outside and catch me a frog."

"A frog?" Jo asked.

"Sure. You cure a cough like this by tying a live

frog to your neck with a string. When the frog dies, the cough is gone."

Jo wrinkled up her nose in disgust. Myrtle was a very puzzling person. A strange combination of folk medicine, superstition, and Shakespeare. "But you told Marcella that frogs are bad luck and that the frogs were a plague on all their houses."

"Did I say that? Well, I guess I did. And they were a plague, you know, to the Fishencors and the Sims."

"But why did you want to scare her like that?"

Myrtle wrinkled up her forehead. "Oh, I didn't start the scaring. Her daddy and Allie were always talking about that bullfrog that scared Marcella's ma and marked up her face." Myrtle smiled. Her gold tooth gleamed. "But I kind of added to the scaring, I guess. I helped it along, you might say."

"But why?"

Myrtle shrugged. "Maybe," she began, "maybe I thought Marcella ought to get out of Goose Creek. And maybe that's the only way I knew to make her get up and go away. After this baby comes, she'll get up and go again. She's making her own luck now. She'll be okay, that girl."

Jo glanced over at Marcella. She was skeptical. Marcella didn't look okay to her. Was Myrtle really capable of delivering a baby? Well, there was nothing Jo could do about it. All she could do was wait.

Two o'clock came. Then three. Marcella was dozing. She was groaning, crying, laughing. Jo wasn't sure. The brandy had made her groggy. She would fall asleep for a few minutes, then the squeaking of the rocker would bring her back to the present.

At last, she heard Myrtle's voice. The voice was urgent and demanding. "Push. Push now, my little lady. You've been dandy. Keep it up. Don't let me down now. Keep pushing!"

Marcella was screaming. Screaming something over and over. Jo's name. Jo jumped up and ran to the bed. Marcella was panting and crying, but she managed to talk, one or two words at a time. "Tell me . . . tell me . . . again . . . it hurts, hurts. Tell about the . . . luck . . . the good luck. Oww, hurts . . . that frogs . . . is good luck. . . . I need . . . that luck. . . . I keep . . . oww . . . seeing frogs . . . them frogs. Hold my hands . . . hold. . . ."

Jo was holding Marcella's hands when the baby's head appeared. It was astonishing to see that a new person was there—whole and complete and just waiting to be pushed out.

She was holding Marcella, holding her own breath. She stared without blinking as Marcella screamed and Myrtle pulled at the base of the head to release the baby's shoulders. Then Jo gagged. The baby— that baby there had something red all over its head and its face. Jo was stunned. No, no, no. Impossible! It was impossible that Marcella's baby should be marked like she was. It couldn't have happened. Couldn't have.

Jo stood frozen to the spot and Myrtle rotated the little body and pulled out the torso and then the bony little legs. Jo gagged again. Everything was red. She couldn't even tell if it was a boy or a

165

girl. Why hadn't Roger just let Ben Fishencor have his way? It wouldn't have hurt Marcella as much as seeing this revolting baby would.

And the red-marked baby was crying already. No one would have to hold it up and slap its bottom. It was outraged. Its tiny, forlorn cry echoed in the wood cabin. Jo felt sick. She was going to vomit. Or faint. She was no longer sure if Marcella was gripping her hands or she was gripping Marcella's.

"Jo, Jo, I need you," Marcella wailed. "I can't look. Tell me."

Jo turned to Myrtle for help, but Myrtle was busy with a towel. She was wiping the pathetic squalling child. Jo blinked. Then she looked harder. As Myrtle daubed at the baby, the red markings seemed to be disappearing. No, that couldn't be. "I'm crazy," Jo thought. "Now I've really gone to pieces." She stood there rigidly.

"The baby," Marcella panted. "Tell me. . . ."

Jo bit down on her tongue. She kept pressing until her top teeth bit through the edge, until she felt a stab of pain, until she tasted the salt of her own blood. The pain brought her back. Myrtle was still washing. The infant was still crying. And the marks *were* washing away. They weren't birthmarks. Just blood. Good, red blood.

"It's a girl," Myrtle crowed, waving the tiny thing in the air. She moved forward and placed it on Marcella's chest. She pulled up the quilt so only the two heads showed. "You have a dandy little girl. You did it."

Marcella smiled weakly. To calm the baby, she patted it on its back. She stroked its fuzzy head. Jo

166

was so busy watching Marcella that it took her a long time to realize that Roger was pounding on the door. Pounding and shouting.

"Let him in," Marcella said softly. "I want him to see my baby. . . . She's mine and of me . . . and I'm naming her Marcella. Never had anything all mine before . . . least nothing that counted."

Jo was about to run over and let Roger in, but Myrtle shook her head. "It's a girl," she yelled, "and you can just keep waiting. A few minutes more won't kill you."

Then Myrtle rolled up the bottom of the quilt and began pressing her hands against Marcella's stomach.

"Oww," Marcella cried out. "No more. Stop. Don't. That hurts."

"Well, it's gonna hurt," Myrtle told her. "But I got to take care of the afterbirth and you've got to be patient with me, girl. You've got to hang on a little longer. Not too bad if you help. And it should be worth it to you. You got your baby—and a lucky one at that."

"Lucky?" Jo asked.

Myrtle smiled. "Born with a veil—a caul on her face. That's good luck."

Jo retreated to a corner while Myrtle finished her work. She didn't attempt to make any logical deductions about Myrtle's words. Good luck—bad luck. Frogs—no frogs. None of it seemed particularly important right now. Marcella had a healthy little girl, and that was what mattered.

At last Myrtle let Jo open the door for Roger. He looked rumpled and dirty. She was sad that he had missed out on the incredible sight of the baby being born. But it was over now. He had missed it. Poor Roger.

He loped across the cabin floor, making the boards jump under his solid gait. Then, as he stood at the edge of the bed with his head cocked, he began grinning. "Look . . . look . . . look!" he shouted.

Jo looked. She saw Marcella's curly hair on the pillow. She saw Marcella's face—a pretty face in spite of the strawberry mark. Why hadn't she ever noticed that before?

"Look! Look!" Roger babbled. "Not at her. At the baby. At the little girl."

Jo looked again. What had she missed? In this half-light, anything was possible. Hard as she tried, she couldn't see anything but the scrunched-up face of the crying baby. She lifted the lamp from the table and held it closer to the bed. Then she let out a gasp. "Her hair!" Jo whispered. "Her hair! My God, the baby has *orange* hair!"

Marcella smiled smugly. "It sure took you long enough," she said. "I done seen that right away."

Chapter 22

≫≫≫ JO AND ROGER WATCHED as Myrtle lined
a willow basket for the little red-haired baby. Marcella was drowsy. Her eyelids kept flapping closed,
then jerking open. The baby was sleeping in her
arms. Jo watched as its towel-wrapped body heaved
up and down with rapid breaths.

"Don't you be taking her away," Marcella pleaded.
"Least not yet." Marcella beckoned to Jo. "Can't
you look her over once more? Take her, Jo, and
look her all over, will you?"

Jo was frightened to take hold of the baby, but
she didn't want to disappoint Marcella. She reached
out. To her dismay, she found that her hands were
trembling as she tried to get hold of the infant. She
felt as if that little head was connected to the body
with rubber bands. It was too fragile for her in-
experienced hands to touch. Gingerly she lifted it
and carried it over to the table.

Somehow she managed to put the baby down
without dropping it. Then, with Roger watching,
she unwrapped it. She examined its wizened but unmarked face, its wrinkled fingers and toes, the bony
legs drawn up to the chest.

"Is Marcy okay? All okay?" Marcella asked,
straining to lift her head from the pillow.

Jo smiled sheepishly. "She's kind of skinny. But
she looks all right, I guess."

Marcella rolled her head back and forth impatiently. "Not that. Can't you see if she's got any marks. Roll her over, will you?"

Jo looked down helplessly. "But I don't know how to," she admitted.

Myrtle bustled over to where Jo stood. "City girl," she scolded. "I saw you. You picked up this precious bundle like she was six pounds of hamburger meat. Now you leave your hands off and I'll roll her over." Myrtle shook her head vehemently. "What a waste of time to be looking for marks. What difference do marks make? If you ask me, you should be out looking for a mouse. . . ."

"For a mouse?" Jo asked.

"Of course, to tie around that baby's neck to keep her from getting sick!"

Marcella sat up. "Not around my baby's neck, you don't. Can't have any dirty old mouse on her neck, you hear?"

Jo smiled. That was the first time she'd ever heard Marcella refuse to take Myrtle's advice. Marcella let herself sink back onto the pillow. "Come on, now. Look on th'other side for marks," she pleaded.

Myrtle nodded. Then, using one big broad hand, she flipped the sleeping baby over on its stomach.

"Look," Roger called out. "There it is."

"What?" Marcella cried fearfully.

"Let me look," Myrtle insisted, bending closer. "Well, so there is. One little mark on the back of her head and neck. But that's nothing. Most everyone born has that."

"Let me see," Marcella pleaded. "I want to see myself."

Myrtle scooped up the baby and brought her to Marcella, holding the infant so Marcella could peer at the back of the head.

"Hey, you know what?" Roger said, loping over to Marcella. "I've got a mark there myself. Chris found it once. Want to see?"

"No," Jo said. "Forget it. We couldn't see anything through all your hair anyway."

Jo moved forward and knelt down so she could look as Marcella looked. Sure enough. There it was. Between the wisps of bright orange hair was a delicate strawberry-colored marking. It was shaped like something familiar.

"A frog!" Marcella giggled. "Can't believe it, but it's shaped like a jumping frog. See them two back legs dangling down the back of the neck?"

Jo laughed. She would have said it looked like a rabbit—a hopping rabbit. But if Marcella wanted to think it looked like a frog . . . well, Jo wasn't going to contradict her.

"It's a good-luck frog, Jo," Marcella whispered happily. "You told me true."

"Enough now," Myrtle insisted, carrying the baby off toward its willow basket. "This girl's got to sleep. Wouldn't hurt you two either. Make up a couple of bedrolls out of quilts and try the front stoop."

"But what about the night air?" Roger asked. "I thought that was supposed to be poisonous."

"'Tis. But that's morning air out there now. Sun'll be up in just a few hours."

There was a noise near the cabin. A rhythmical noise. Footsteps, maybe. Heavy boots tramping. Jo was curled up on the porch in a comfortable bed-roll. It took great effort for her to open her eyes. She looked over at Roger. His eyes were open and he was already sitting up. Jo sat up too. Then she and Roger both peered through the early-morning gray-ness, trying to locate the source of the tramping noise.

It was coming closer. Right up to where they sat. Then they saw him. It was Ben Fishencor coming up the hill and heading straight for the cabin. He was still dressed in his tuxedo. A wilted flower hung from his buttonhole. His patent-leather pumps had been replaced by heavy work boots, but otherwise his dress was unchanged from the night before. He was unshaven. His face looked bluish in the predawn dimness but still coldly handsome. His chin was thrust out; his eyes glared from under their heavy brows.

Jo held her breath. She was afraid. She remembered the wedding and his threats about Marcella. She was too frightened to look over at Roger, but she sensed that he, too, was rigid and tense.

Ben Fishencor didn't say a word to either one of them. He stared at them in silence for a long instant. Then he pushed between them and approached the door of the cabin. He forced it open with one kick of his boot.

Jo and Roger both stood up. This unshaven man was the violent, crazy person who had threatened to kill her only hours before. Without a word, they followed Ben Fishencor into the cabin.

Myrtle was sitting at the table with her head down. The coronet of braids was resting on her fore-arms. She was snoring softly.

Marcella was in bed, but she was not sleeping. She was awake, staring at her father with unblinking eyes. He stood with both fists clenched behind his back. Jo edged over slightly, so she could see his face. His eyes were darting back and forth rapidly. First he would look at Marcella and then at the baby in the basket.

In this dim light, Jo wondered, could he see well enough to make out that head of orange hair? She squinted. No, probably not. Jo felt shaky. Perhaps she didn't have enough adrenalin left for one more crisis. She couldn't seem to think or act. Now she would just stand there and watch Ben Fishencor kill his daughter and kill her new baby.

But Roger was alert. He had already taken hold of an empty brandy bottle. He stood with it poised behind Ben Fishencor's head, ready to strike him if necessary. Nothing was happening yet; Marcella and her father were just exchanging cold, mute stares. But Roger was there, ready to be heroic again. Jo wanted to laugh as this odd melodrama unfolded.

Finally Marcella spoke. Her voice was quiet but firm. "Roger, you go on and put down that bottle, you hear? Leave him be. You won't need no bottle."

Ben Fishencor didn't even bother to turn around to see what Marcella was referring to. Roger lowered the bottle, but he didn't put it down. Instead, he stood there clutching it with two hands.

Then Marcella spoke again. "Daddy, I done had a little girl last night. You'll like her a lot because she's a beauty. A red-haired beauty."

"I can see," her father said, knocking a clod of mud from one boot.

Marcella propped herself up on one elbow. "I thought maybe you'd be happy since she's all beautiful instead of like me." She paused, waiting for some kind of answer from him, but he didn't speak.

Marcella frowned. "But you don't care none. None at all. You know what? I'm done trying to please you—done waiting on you, trying to make you care for me like Allie. You always said we shared things." Marcella paused for a deep breath. Then she continued. "Oh, we shared, but she always got the best part. She got the white meat and I got the tail. She got the piece of cake with the rose on it. You thought I was bad luck, that it was my fault about the bakery—that people stopped buying on account of me. You was always took with shame over me and my mark."

Marcella spoke calmly and softly. Jo had never heard her talk so much at one time. Ben Fishencor stood there glaring and silent. After a short pause, Marcella went on. "Maybe Mama got sick and died because she thought she wasn't good enough for you since she got so fat. Poor Mama—with you always singing out about your daughter Allie and how pretty she was and all."

After a short pause, Marcella continued. "I tried everything to please you. To bring you good luck, to make you care; but nothing worked. And no one was ever nice to me after Mama went except Myrtle sometimes. And then Pepper. But I weren't nothing special to him. He's that nice to everybody. He even gave me a buckeye and a sweatshirt, too. Did you know that?"

"It's all the frogs," Ben Fishencor said. "All the goddamned frogs!"

Marcella shook her head. "You kept telling me about Mama and the frogs and that these frogs here was a plague. It was just to scare me—just to keep me at home so no one'd see me. So I could scrub and mop and be waiting on you. You never did mind that. The frogs ain't no plague and no bad luck. Well, maybe for you, but not for me. They's just a lot of helpless little things hopping about."

Ben Fishencor narrowed his eyes until they were only slits. "Get out," he said. "I don't ever want to see you again. Bad enough for you to come back pregnant. But now you and that damned orange-headed baby are going to make me and Allie the laughingstock of Goose Creek." He glanced over toward the baby. "Now you get out before I change my mind and kill you both."

Jo could see that Roger was raising the bottle again. But he didn't bring it down on the back of Ben Fishencor's head. He just stood there.

"What will people think—that's all you ever did think of," Marcella said. "I'm going, don't worry, and I'll be lucky to be rid of the whole pack of you. I'm going to leave you to the frogs. Hope they crawl in your bed at night and make you squirm."

"I would have killed you last night, Marcella. What do you want? For me to do it now?"

Marcella rolled over on her side and looked over to the baby's basket. "You can do it now if you want. But you can't touch her. I'll raise up out of this bed or out of my grave and strangle you if you touch her. Now, kill me, will you? Or go away and leave me be." With these words, she closed her eyes and locked her fingers together over the stomach that had held the baby.

Ben Fishencor didn't move. He just stood there staring. "I always wondered," he said, "if you was mine. If I could have fathered a baby marked up like you. . . ." Only a twitch of Marcella's upper lip betrayed that she had heard his words. She kept her eyes firmly closed.

At this moment, Myrtle raised her head up from the table. "Okay," she commanded, waving impatiently at Ben Fishencor, "you've had your say, old man. Now get!"

Jo watched tensely as Ben gave Marcella one more searching look. His unshaven face didn't look so handsome now, with its jaw hanging loose in defeat.

After a long moment, he turned and stomped out of the cabin. Marcella opened her eyes and looked over toward the baby again.

Jo moved closer and sat down on the edge of the bed. "But weren't you afraid, Marcella?" she asked. "How could you talk to him like that?"

Marcella smiled vaguely. "Oh, there weren't no danger," she mused. "He's a proud man. But he always was a coward."

Chapter 23

ろろろ JO AND ROGER WERE SITTING on the steps
of the cabin waiting for the sun to come up. Beads
of dew clung to the grass and wildflowers. To Jo,
everything looked so fresh and new. Beyond their hill,
the sun was about to rise. They could see a rose-
colored glow in the sky. But where they were sitting,
it was still dim and chilly.

Jo was wide awake. She kept talking to Roger in
a low voice. About how scared she was when Ben
Fishencor stomped into the cabin. About watching
the birth of Marcella's baby. She told him what she'd
seen and how she'd felt. How brave and wonderful
Marcella had been. That she had forgotten to look
and see how Myrtle had tied off the umbilical cord.
Jo knew she was repeating herself, but she couldn't
seem to stop.

"What if . . ." Roger interrupted finally, "what if
Myrtle hadn't come?"

Jo's face sobered. "Well . . . I could have handled
it. Somehow, I would have managed. Maybe."

She looked at Roger and noticed that he was
rubbing his hands together to ward off the chill.
Strange that he should be cold. She didn't feel cold
at all.

"Everything looks so beautiful this morning," she
sighed, looking around again. "Yet it happens every
day. Babies are born. The sun comes up. The birds

sing. Look at the cardinal on that branch up there. The red is so strong it looks synthetic. And that bird does this every morning, even when we're not here to listen. . . ."

Roger yawned. "For weeks, you bitched about how awful Marcella was. Now you rhapsodize about how superlative she is and everything around her. Sometimes," he added, "you bore me."

Jo looked up again to the cardinal and beyond him to the egg-yolk sun oozing up beyond the hill. She bit down on her bottom lip. She ran one hand through her tangled hair. But she didn't answer. She didn't even try.

For a long time, they sat there without speaking. The sun was inching higher, tinting everything pink. At last, Roger broke the silence. "The frogs. You haven't studied them at all since we came. Do you think it's really a plague?"

"I don't know," Jo answered slowly. "I don't really care, either."

"But, without the frogs, you never would have met Marcella and come here at all."

Jo nodded. "That's true."

Roger grinned. "It was *some* adventure, wasn't it? Wait 'til our folks hear. Maybe we'll even come back some other time. Wouldn't you like to find out more about Marcella? How she got involved with Pepper? Why Pepper married Allie instead? Aren't you curious?"

Jo shook her head. "Not particularly."

"Would Marcella ever marry Pepper if she had the chance? I mean, if Pepper and Allie should get divorced or something. Do you think Ben Fishencor will make trouble for her up in the city? And then there's Myrtle. Don't you wonder about her, too? Why does she take such an interest in the Fishencor family? How she can seem to be so ordinary and still do extraordinary things—like delivering babies? Are you listening to me, Jo?"

"I'm listening," Jo said.

"Then what's wrong with you? Where's your curiosity? Have you lost your adventurous spirit?"

"No," Jo replied firmly. "No, I haven't."

"Well, then," Roger said, "we'll have to ask Marcella what we can do. Maybe we could help— arrange a secret meeting between her and Pepper. After all, he might want to see little Marcy. She *is* his daughter."

Jo smiled and shook her head again. "No! Can't you hear me? I told you I'm not interested."

"What's wrong with you this morning?"

"Nothing's wrong," Jo insisted. "I just don't seem to be thinking like you're thinking—or interested in the things that interest you."

Roger frowned. "What about when we get back to the city? We'll still play tennis, won't we?"

"I guess so. Maybe. If I have time. I have the Maypole coming up and then final exams. We'll see. . . ."

Roger stood up abruptly and put his hands on his hips. "Then tell me what's important to you now? At least answer that for me!"

Jo looked around. The pink tint was fading from the air. Now the sun was looking yellow instead of brilliant orange. Clouds that had seemed to be on fire only moments ago were now a dark gray. Before her, she saw green hills and the wooden outhouse with its splintery door hanging ajar. Then she spoke. "The message from the outhouse, I guess. That's important."

"The message from the outhouse?" Roger asked. "Which one?"

Jo looked over toward the pump. She noticed that there was one small, brown frog sitting in the damp mud under its spout. Then she turned back to Roger. " 'There are more things in heaven and earth,' " she said, " 'than are dreamt of in your philosophy.' "

Roger shook one finger at her. "That's heavy stuff," he said. "And you left out the 'Horatio,' just like Myrtle did."

Jo smiled. "Yes . . . well, you're right. But that's not the important part of the message, is it?"

⇔⇔   ⇔⇔

ABOUT THE AUTHOR

SUSAN TERRIS received her B.A. at Wellesley College and her M.A. in English Literature at San Francisco State College. She is the author of many articles and short stories for children. She has also written several books, including *The Drowning Boy, On Fire, The Upstairs Witch and the Downstairs Witch,* and *The Backwards Boots*. Mrs. Terris and her husband, David, a stockbroker, live in San Francisco with their three children: Danny, Michael, and Amy.